A HARD FALL

Gunfire slashed through the cottonwoods. McCan aimed, but the forms shifted and he did not know friend from assailant.

Someone cursed; a rifle fired. McCan pushed upward, over the rock, but his foot slid on the damp ground and he crashed down hard. His head struck something, night closed in, and he was out.

He came to moments, maybe an hour later. His head was bloody and throbbed. He struggled for perspective. He pushed up on his forearms and looked across the campsite, and suddenly his view was blocked by what appeared to be twin tree trunks. Focusing, he saw they were legs. His eyes lifted—a rifle butt descended toward his face . . .

ST. MARTIN'S PAPERBACKS TITLES
BY CAMERON JUDD

THE GLORY RIVER
SNOW SKY
CORRIGAN
TIMBER CREEK

Coming in December:

TEXAS FREEDOM

TIMBER CREEK

CAMERON JUDD

St. Martin's Paperbacks

TIMBER CREEK

Copyright © 1989 by Cameron Judd.
Excerpt from *The Glory River* copyright © 1998 by Cameron Judd.

ISBN: 0-312-96767-5

Printed in the United States of America

Bantam edition / May 1989
St. Martin's Paperbacks edition / November 1998

10 9 8 7 6 5 4 3 2 1

To Rhonda

PART I

DEADWOOD

CHAPTER 1

—

As Luke McCan strode through the gate of the Tolliver & McClelland freight yard, a black man scrubbing mud from a wagon turned to watch him. McCan nodded a greeting, but the big fellow gave not even a grunt in return.

At the doorway of the unpainted building of rough lumber, McCan took off his hat. Shifting it in his hands, he tried to swallow his tension; he couldn't. He straightened his shoulders and walked inside.

It was dark there, and musty. McCan stood blind a couple of moments as his eyes adjusted. He found himself facing three somber men on a bench against the opposite wall. They slumped more than sat, expressionless as tomcats. McCan nodded, and got no more reaction than he had from the man outside. Like wooden Indians in a cigar store, he thought.

"Could you tell me where I'd find Ira Tolliver?" he asked.

Wooden Indian number three raised a hand-rolled smoke to his lips and took a slow drag as he tilted his head toward a door at the far corner of the room. It was ajar, and beyond it McCan saw the corner of a big pigeonholed desk, as cluttered as a postmaster's, and an equally paper-laden oaken filing cabinet. He nodded his thanks and headed for the door.

Inside the office sat a fat man with an unlit cigar stub jutting over an impressive collection of chins. He looked up; the chins danced gelatinously beneath broad jowls.

"What is it?" he gruffly asked.

"Are you Ira Tolliver?"

"I am."

"I'd like to speak to you a moment."

The man shrugged, and McCan entered. The office was cramped, and looked as if it had never been cleaned. It was a refuge for stray odors. Tolliver shuffled papers as McCan looked for a seat. The businessman's rubbery mouth wrapped itself around the well-chewed cigar, a duplicate of any one of a score of others that lay about on the floor.

McCan evicted an ancient gray tabby from a chair and took its place, then waited until Tolliver turned his somnolent gaze to him.

"You got business?"

"My name is Luke McCan. I'm looking for work."

"Uh-huh. Somebody say I'm hiring?"

"No, sir. I just figured to ask."

Tolliver dug out a match and lit his cigar. Through the smoke, his face was that of a bulldog, fat and lazy. "What work you after?"

"I'd like to be a teamster." He anticipated the follow-up question. "I've got experience—I hauled freight in Missouri almost a year."

"Oxen?"

"Mules."

"We use oxen." Tolliver looked to his papers again,

4

conversation concluded. The cigar made a four-inch roll to the other side of his mouth.

"I can drive oxen, Mr. Tolliver. I've done it a time or two, and I can pick up what I don't already know."

"How long you been in Pierre, son?"

"About a week."

"Where are you from?"

"St. Louis."

"You're young."

"Twenty-five. I'm told I look younger."

"You got folks?"

"No parents. They died just over a year ago, a wagon accident. I've got one sister living in Independence."

"What brought you to Dakota?"

"I just wanted to come, and saw no reason not to."

"You know where my freight line runs, son?"

"Deadwood, I hear."

"That's right. Black Hills. Gold country. A lot of young bucks looking for a way to get there." He leaned back in his chair; it creaked and moaned as if in pain. McCan caught his implication and shook his head.

"I'm not looking for a ticket to Deadwood," he said. "If I wanted to go there, I'd get on my horse and ride." He didn't mention he had lost his horse in a poker bet a week ago.

Tolliver flipped an ash. "This line cuts through Sioux country. There's highwaymen too. We got a one-mile-wide right-of-way through to Deadwood, but that don't mean a lot to the lower types. And Deadwood, once you get there, is about as dangerous as the trail."

"I'll try to take care of myself."

"Bill Hickok tried too. He's moldering in his grave on Mount Moriah."

McCan saw Tolliver was trying hard to sell him on *not* deserting the freight line in Deadwood. It was not something he had thought of doing, but all this talk was making him wonder if he *should.*

"I'm just looking for a job," McCan said. "Can you use me?"

Tolliver pondered. "A teamster quit me last week, and we got a shipment going out Monday. You come back in a couple of days, and we'll start breaking you in."

They talked pay, shook hands, and McCan left. He headed to a café and, in celebration, ordered a steak, biscuits, and coffee. As he ate, he looked out the café window at the busy street.

Pierre stood at the bend of the Missouri in the southern Dakota Territory. Since the discovery of gold in the Black Hills, the freight business out of Pierre had flourished, for the Black Hills had only two links to the world beyond: freight lines and stagecoaches. By those conduits people and goods were funneled into the Black Hills, and carried out again were stories of goldmining towns such as Deadwood. Talk had it that Deadwood was a place of intense living and easily found death. The murder of Wild Bill Hickok there a few years back had only bolstered the gritty mystique of the town.

McCan sipped coffee and tilted his chair back against the wall. He was a slender man and rather tall, his features smooth and appealing if not outright handsome. He dressed well for one who had been without a job for a year; his inheritance from his parents had been modest, but enough to finance a few months of wandering. He should invest what was left in something practical, he knew, but such was not his way. He had dreamed of roaming like this from the first time he'd toddled across his nursery. Had he not gambled away his horse, he might have been content to remain jobless a bit longer; applying for work with Tolliver had been a momentary inspiration, a way to get in a little more travel with no investment of his own money.

Now McCan was thinking of Deadwood, and wondering why he had not thought of it before. Tolliver, in his eagerness to steer his thoughts from it, had instead turned them to it.

McCan left the café and walked without aim along the street. In front of a store whose window sign read MINING TOOLS—HIGH QUALITY AND LOW PRICE, he paused to roll a cigarette. The door opened and a man emerged, arms filled with supplies. Blinded by his load, he walked directly into McCan, and tools and other goods fell all around.

The man cursed, but it was directed at the situation rather than McCan, so McCan took no offense.

"If I had seen you coming, I would have moved," McCan said.

"Not your fault."

"Let me help you," McCan said. He and the man picked up the items and loaded them into a small covered wagon parked by the curb of the boardwalk.

McCan thrust out his hand and said his name. The other man took the hand and said, "I'm Caleb Black. I'm obliged for your help."

McCan gestured toward the wagon. "You're bound for Deadwood?"

"Like everybody else."

"I'm heading that way myself. I'm a teamster for the Tolliver company yonder. Just hired on."

"Maybe I'll see you in the Black Hills then."

"Maybe so."

Caleb Black climbed to his seat and rode away. Luke McCan watched him depart, then looked westward toward the horizon that hid the Black Hills.

McCan wrote a letter that night by candlelight.

Mrs. Martha Hyatt
Independence, Missouri

My Dear Martha,

As I write you now, I'm a teamster. When you hear from me next, I likely will be a gold miner in the town of Deadwood. That is where the freight line that has given me a job runs, and likely I will stay on once we get there, for it is the talk of everyone I see. There is money to be made there at honest labor, and I will be glad to make my part.

Our father would have been proud of me, would he not? "Make a living with the sweat of your brow" always was his theme—with me at least—though as a female you probably were spared some of that, it being more your duty to marry well, in his eyes, than to work hard. You've done both.

It is late and I will not write you long, but you will hear again from me when I am settled at the Black Hills mines. To answer the question of your last letter: no, I have not gambled away all my inheritance, though I have kept to my poker-playing ways. I see no harm in it, though I know in your eyes it is the fatal vice that will ruin my life, if not damn my soul, for you were well-taught by Mother about the wicked ways of men.

But do not worry about me, and be sure you will
hear from me soon

> Your affectionate brother,
> Luke

CHAPTER 2

McCan labored through Saturday night, filling canvas sacks, heaving crates, stacking goods, covering the loaded wagons with tarpaulins. It was grueling work, with more to come on Sunday, for the loading was behind schedule.

McCan worked with Bob Webster, the black man he had seen washing wagons in the freight yard. Webster was talkative now, warmed to McCan through the brotherhood of labor. McCan asked questions, and Webster answered them in detail.

Tolliver, he said, would not come along on the journey. He was a businessman—at home behind a desk, but a stranger to a freight wagon seat. Ira Tolliver had founded the company three years before with a man named Zeke McClelland, and the latter had actually led the freight runs. McClelland had died after the first year, and Tolliver had kept the company running alone, amid rumors that he had swindled McClelland's widow. Now the freight runs were led by an employee named Benjamin Weaver.

Webster pointed Weaver out to McCan; he was thin-featured, with a mustache that drooped around fleshless lips. The left side of his face was ballooned incessantly with hot-twist tobacco. But he never spat; Webster claimed he swallowed the juice as if it were sugar water.

"Weaver is a good man to have leading," Webster said. "Better than Zeke McClelland was on his best day. Listen to him and you'll learn a lot about this business."

On Sunday the crew headed to the plains north of town to round up and herd in the oxen grazing there. It was easy; the oxen were accustomed to the process and all but fell into line. They plodded willingly back to the freight yard, where they were penned in a make-shift corral. Webster and McCan watered them and gave them hay, and the big beasts consumed both in placid contentment, watching the crew finish preparations for the Monday run.

Webster began McCan's education in the freight business. He gave a rapid-fire description of the train: ten teams of twenty oxen, each team pulling three wagons hitched together, each wagon carefully weighted. Lead wagons would carry seven thousand pounds, middle or swing wagons about five thousand each, and trail wagons about three thousand.

Before dawn Monday the train began its roll toward the Missouri. Ben Weaver led, followed by McCan. McCan sat astride his lead wagon, traces in his hands and the whoops and curses of the teamsters behind him ringing in his ears. The earth made a sodden, crushing noise beneath the big wheels of the wagons. As the sky turned from black to lavender to pale gold, a sense of adventure filled McCan.

The wagons reached the Missouri, and Weaver halted his team near the ferry that would convey the entire train across. Morning rays splintered over the river's chopped surface, brightening as the sun rose. Weaver's figure etched itself against the silver background as he talked to the long-bearded ferryman. McCan threw the brake and leaned back, knowing the crossing would be slow.

Indeed, it was almost noon before the chuck wagon at the end of the train was parked across the water, with a huge kettle of stew bubbling beside it. None of the teamsters had eaten that morning, because of the early departure from Pierre, so they accepted the food with the eagerness of dying souls grasping a sacrament.

Webster sat beside McCan, who was propped against a wheel of his swing wagon. Webster pulled away his hat and wiped the sweat off with his sleeve. "Mighty hot," he said.

"It is. How long will we stay here?"

"Most all day. The oxen can't take a lot of heat. We'll travel from the later part of the afternoon until we can't see no more. Then we'll camp, get up before dawn, and roll until it gets hot tomorrow. Good thing about this business is, you don't work much the hot part of the day. The bad part is, you don't get breakfast until about noon."

"How many miles will we cover a day?"

"It depends on the ground and the weather. On a good day, maybe almost twenty miles. On a bad one, maybe five or six."

McCan swatted a fly on his knee. "Slow way to get to Deadwood."

Webster looked at him sidewise. "You in a particular hurry?"

"I don't suppose. But I hear it's quite a place."

Webster smiled vaguely. "Oh, it is. You thinking of becoming a miner, maybe?"

"Would I tell you if I was?"

"There's nothing wrong with mining," Webster said. "A man sure can't get rich driving a team of oxen."

McCan had a sudden insight. "You're not coming back, are you, Webster?"

Webster's dark eyes flickered around. "Don't say that so loud. Old Weaver listens for such, and there's the devil to pay if he hears. I've thought of leaving, sure, but it can be hard for a colored man to get work if the mining goes bust. I can't let go of what I've got without a lot of thinking."

They passed the hot hours around the wagons. Men napped, smoked, talked among themselves. Except Ben Weaver; he stayed alone, staring at nothing, whittling a stick of pine.

"He's always like that," Webster said. "Either he's had some hard times in his life, or one of these oxen kicked him in the head. He's a smart man and a good leader, but he's always alone."

When the afternoon waned, the teamsters yoked up and rolled out. The oxen were full and rested and made good time. Weaver's wagon left deep ruts behind, so McCan pulled off his trail. Others behind him did the same, and soon the train stretched a quarter of a mile long and a sixth of a mile wide.

Dark came, but the sky was clear and moonlit. Weaver called back to McCan, and he in turn passed the message back: "Clear night! Roll on!"

Roll they did, a good two hours past dark. Such a thing was rare, McCan would learn. Usually darkness marked the end of the working day.

The wagons finally halted, and the oxen were freed to graze. Leftover stew was served, bedrolls came out, and Harvey Lane, the night guard, emerged from his sleeper wagon, which trailed along after Webster's wagons. He went to work as the others lay down, and sleep swept in with the song of crickets and the whisper of grass.

Lane's jarring call awakened McCan just before dawn. He crawled out, longing for coffee, knowing there would be none until they were far down the trail.

It was while the teamsters yoked their oxen under the paling sky that the first hint of trouble came.

CHAPTER 3

It was a freakish event, but it set off hard feelings that had stewed, mostly unnoticed, for months.

Webster was yoking two oxen when Roy Sturley, a teamster from Arkansas, passed him. One of Webster's oxen moved suddenly and threw him off balance. Webster staggered back against Sturley, who dropped a yoke he had been carrying. It hit his foot.

Sturley spat, "Watch yourself, nigger!" and threw a hard right against Webster's jaw.

Webster squarely faced the man who had uttered and done what he would tolerate from no one. Sturley stared back, brushed dirt from his sleeve, and breathed loudly through his teeth.

"Nobody calls me that, Sturley," Webster said.

The teamsters gathered. Some grinned, others looked worried. McCan edged in and touched Webster's shoulder; Webster pulled away as if it burned him.

From the other side of the circle emerged Jimmy Wyatt, one of the youngest teamsters. He was a short, slight fellow with flame-orange hair and a ruddy face dotted with pancake freckles. He looked at McCan and said, "Stay out of it. It ain't right for a nigger to push a man."

"It was the ox moving that done it," somebody said.

"No. He pushed me a-purpose," Sturley interjected. "You seen it, didn't you, Jimmy?"

"Sure did."

McCan turned to Bob Webster. "Bob, just walk away from it."

Webster glared at him. "Shut up, Luke. I fight my own fights."

"Listen at that!" Wyatt chortled. "You gonna let a nigger talk that way to you?"

McCan was going to respond, but suddenly Sturley lunged forward, swinging wildly. Several blows connected against Webster's neck, chest, and jaw. A gout of blood squirted as a final swing hammered his nose. He fell back, and Wyatt whooped in tent-revival ecstasy.

Webster recovered quickly. He threw himself on his opponent, slammed a hard fist against his eye, and pounded a left into his gut. Sturley grunted, cursed, and groped for Webster's neck. He gripped it and squeezed until his fingernails were white, but Webster seemed unaware of the hands at his throat.

The black man pounded two more bruising punches into Sturley's stomach, then brought up his fists and spread them between Sturley's forearms, knocking the hands from his neck. He heaved forward, head lowered, and butted a granite forehead against Sturley's skull. The crack was like mountain goats colliding.

Sturley fell, but rose with a knife in his hand.

"Yeah!" Wyatt exulted. "Cut him!"

The men nearest Sturley parted suddenly, like a stand of wheat divided by a twister. Weaver came through the gap, walked up to Sturley, and punched his jaw with one hand while deftly taking the knife with the other. Sturley fell back two steps, then looked into the train leader's cold eyes. His face flared livid, then drained to funeral-parlor white.

"But the darky pushed me," he said feebly.

"Bob's my best teamster," Weaver said. "I won't have you cutting him up. And as for you, Bob, I won't tolerate troublemaking or folks with chips on their shoulders. The rest of you, clear out. We're losing time."

Sturley straightened and turned to Webster. The two stared like wary cats as Weaver walked away, confident from experience that his warning was enough to end the fight.

The atmosphere crackled with back-and-forth tension until at last Sturley turned away, muttering. Webster watched him go, then dug out his handkerchief and wiped away the blood. The other teamsters scattered, knowing Weaver meant what he said.

Webster returned to his oxen. McCan thought of going to him, but didn't. He hitched his own team and awaited the order to roll.

The journey continued until the sun raged hot. They stopped the wagons, and the cook provided beans seasoned with big hunks of bacon. The men lined up with pewter bowls in hand; McCan fell in behind Webster.

The cook, Sterling Slater, dished out huge portions and fat biscuits. When Webster received his, he stared first at his bowl, then at Slater.

"Where's the rest?" he demanded.

"What are you talking about?" Slater's confusion was justified, for he had given Webster the same amount as the others.

"You heard me."

Slater twitched thick brows and emphatically spit a

dollop of tobacco juice earthward, but he dished out an extra heap for Webster, who then stepped down the line. He was a volcano seething toward explosion.

Jimmy Wyatt thrust his bowl under Slater's nose. "Fill it up. As much as the nigger got."

McCan's eyes darted to Webster. The big teamster sat with his back toward him, shoveling beans into his mouth. He hadn't heard, or at least didn't let on.

For two days there was no further trouble. Webster calmed down, but remained brooding and distant. McCan spoke to him only a little, for most of the time it was obvious Webster wanted to be left alone.

Rain came, and the going was slow. The daily mileage dropped to six, and often the wagons had to be pushed through mud. Streams swelled to twice normal size, and Weaver worried aloud about the Cheyenne River farther on.

On the fourth day out from Pierre, the train encountered an emigrant wagon beside a stream. McCan recognized it as Caleb Black's.

"Stuck trying to cross?" he asked Weaver.

"Could be. Or maybe redskins, or bandits. If you know this fellow, come with me."

As they drew near, McCan pointed out two dead mules lying nearby in blackened blood, covered with flies.

"He was jumped for sure," Weaver said. "Keep a sharp eye."

McCan could see now that the wagon had bullet holes in the sides and rips in the canvas. From inside it a voice rang out: "Hold it there—come around where I can see your faces."

It was Caleb Black's voice, coming over the long barrel of a Henry that jutted out of the wagon. McCan and Weaver raised their hands.

"Easy, friend," Weaver said. "We're teamsters, here to help you if you need it."

The flaps moved and Black peered over the tailgate. He lowered the Henry. "Come on, then."

He stepped from the wagon as they approached. He recognized McCan, even remembered his name.

"Redskins?" Weaver asked.

"No, white men. Dressed like redskins to try to fool me, but I seen their faces. I'll know them when I see them again."

Weaver said, "You won't see them. Most of the highwaymen keep hid out. A few turn up in Deadwood from time to time—Tom Branton and Evan Bridger, mostly. Nobody bothers them. The law has no proof on them, and most folks are scared of them."

Black snorted contemptuously. "I'll teach 'em scared!"

"You can ride into Deadwood with us," Weaver said. "We'll hitch your wagon behind McCan's team. You can pay your way as an assistant night guard, or by helping the cook, or whatever."

"I'm obliged."

They tied on Black's wagon and moved on; Black rode in the seat beside McCan. The sun grew hot, and the oxen slowed after a few miles. At last Weaver signaled the halt.

CHAPTER 4

——

When they stopped, Caleb Black crawled inside his wagon and went to sleep. By then, McCan had received a nutshell history of Black and kin.

Black's brother, Walter, was already mining in the Black Hills, and had invited Caleb to join him. The brothers had one younger sister, who lived in Minnesota with her husband, a farmer. Caleb hoped to persuade them to join him in Deadwood after he became settled with Walter.

He answered McCan's questions: No, he had not mined before. Yes, he had read all about it. No, Walter was not rich—not yet. But yes, he would be, and Caleb too. He was sure of it.

The rains stopped, but the mucky land—called gumbo by the veteran teamsters—continued to hamper· their progress. The Cheyenne, however, had receded by the time they reached it, and fording was easy. From there on the journey went speedily.

The first sight of the Black Hills reconfirmed to McCan his plan to stay. From a distance they truly were black, because of the pine and spruce on their summits. They crumpled the land like a scuffed-up carpet for a hundred miles on the western border of the territory, down to the Badlands farther south. At places, the hills humped like knuckles or pointed like fingers at the sky.

They approached Deadwood through the Centennial Prairie, where the oxen would graze after the wagons were unloaded. There would be only one day of rest and one night of carousing in Deadwood before the trip back to Pierre—a trip McCan would not make.

McCan had picked up some of Deadwood's history along the way. The town had been founded in 1875, after the discovery of gold there, and at first had been called Deadwood Gulch. The latter title was appropriate; the town was bordered by hills, and thus had grown in a long strand. Along its rutted course sprouted businesses—some legitimate, others not. There were those who called Deadwood the Gomorrah of the west.

Deadwood prospered. The Black Hills swarmed with prospectors; the town was populated with those who made a living, in a variety of ways, off the earnings brought in by the miners.

Deadwood had a decidedly lawless streak, and every kind of human castoff infested its alleyways and dark corners. Prostitutes, gamblers, thieves, murderers— they were plentiful in this hell-pit of a town, and many were those who predicted that one day the Almighty would swallow Deadwood into the bowels of the land and be done with it. The straight and narrow did not pass within a hundred miles of the Black Hills. Deadwood was a rough and cruel town, a place men did not go if they valued their mortal lives and immortal souls. Naturally enough, it was crowded.

The freight wagons rolled into Deadwood late in the afternoon. Unloading them proved difficult and slow. McCan had time only to glance over the town before the return to camp. The narrow street was little more than a wide gully with squatty buildings along it, all of them drab and crude, some consisting more of canvas than lumber.

McCan noted Carl Mann's Saloon, supposedly one of the wildest in town, where Jack McCall had blown out Bill Hickok's brains. They had buried Wild Bill behind the saloon at first, but later moved him to Mount Moriah, overlooking the town. He had plenty of company there; violent death happened frequently in Deadwood. "When the gold pans out," Webster observed, "they can start mining lead out of the corpses on the hill."

Weaver didn't hand out pay until the teamsters were back on the Centennial Prairie; it was his way of making sure they returned. A few slipped back to town immediately, but McCan was exhausted from the day's work. He crawled into his bedroll and fell asleep.

Caleb Black had remained in town. McCan thought about him just before he went to sleep. Probably he was looking for his brother right now. A stake waiting for him—a lucky man.

In the morning, McCan and Webster took two horses from the train remuda and rode into town. Weaver stayed behind with the wagons, ostensibly to guard them, but McCan figured that for an excuse. Weaver seemingly had no need for recreation or release, even company. He was a mystery McCan never would solve, for he knew when he waved his goodbye to him he would see him no more.

McCan and Webster sought out Hardin Crowley, a fellow teamster Webster said was honest, and gave him payment for the horses. "Take it back to Weaver when you leave," McCan said. "We'll not be thought horse thieves by any man."

Crowley pocketed the money. "Good luck to both of you," he said. "Next run, I'll be staying on myself. Wish I could now."

They left their horses at a livery and took to the street. Webster said there were days Deadwood was lifeless as its name, others when it teemed even at noon. This was one of the latter.

Men walked the boardwalks and muddy street, horses milled about, wagons creaked by, merchants sat in the doorways of their shops or tended customers inside. It was an incredible jumble, alternately thrilling and exhausting to observe. As the sun rose, the drab town took on a surreal light that made it almost beautiful, in a primitive way.

McCan stopped; approaching from the other end of the street were Sturley and Wyatt. He felt Webster bristle.

The pair approached and stopped, keeping out of reach of Webster's long arms. Wyatt grinned cockily. "You're keeping some bad company, McCan."

McCan said nothing. Wyatt and Sturley smelled like whiskey, even at this early hour. Wyatt weaved where he stood.

"Can't you talk?" Wyatt said. "It ain't polite to stand and stare at a man like a bug-eyed jackass."

"Just move aside and don't cause trouble," McCan said.

Wyatt presented a look of offended innocence. "Trouble? Did I talk about trouble, Roy? We're just trying to be nice. We're nice to everybody. Even to niggers like you, boy. I'm talking to you, Webster."

Webster moved almost imperceptibly, but managed to squelch whatever he was about to do or say. Wyatt saw he had touched a nerve. He grinned broadly.

"What's the matter, black boy? I make you mad?"

Webster nodded. "You did." His hand flashed out with amazing celerity, and his whole body lunged like a rattler's to within striking distance. Bone crunched horribly as Wyatt's nose went flat under Webster's fist. He grasped his injured face; tears poured out to mix with blood. Sturley gaped, open-mouthed and silent, at his injured partner, who now sat on his rump in the street with blood gushing down his shirt.

Wyatt struggled to his feet again, gripping his nose. He pointed at Webster and said, "You're dead, nigger."

His hand fell to the ivory-handled Colt he always wore. He drew and leveled it, clicked the hammer, and aimed the pistol between Webster's eyes.

McCan pushed the barrel aside as Wyatt squeezed the trigger. There was an empty click. Wyatt raised the pistol and stared crazily at it.

Webster laughed. "They don't work unloaded," he said. He kicked upward and caught Wyatt full force in the groin. Wyatt's body rose a foot off the street and fell backward. His eyes bleared; he tried to scream, but couldn't. As for Sturley, he backed off, then ran.

Webster knelt beside Wyatt and gently took the pistol from his hand. "I unloaded this while you slept the night after you decided mine and Sturley's business was yours. I never take a chance with a fool. And I figured you to be fool enough not to bother to check your own pistol before you came to town. You won't make it here, Wyatt. There's men what can eat you alive."

Webster tossed the pistol into an alley. A drunk scurried to it, stooped, then he and the pistol were gone.

Webster stood and he and McCan walked away. Sturley was gone. Wyatt still writhed in the dirt.

"It isn't over, Bob," McCan said.

"I know it." Webster paused. "Maybe I ought to get me a pistol."

"Both of us," McCan said.

They heard laughter, and McCan turned. A tall man with graying hair and a leathery face stood in the doorway of a tent saloon, a painted girl under his arm and a beer in his hand. He laughed at McCan and Webster, and when McCan looked at him, raised his beer in salute. The man turned back into the dark saloon interior.

"Who was that?" McCan asked. But Webster didn't know.

CHAPTER 5

The gunseller was a small man with a monocle; he smiled throughout the entire transaction. "Good choices indeed," he said as he passed two Colts over the countertop. "It's been a good day for Mr. Colt. I sold a pistol identical to these earlier today—only minutes before you arrived."

Webster and McCan exchanged a glance. "Let me guess—a shrimpy little fellow with a busted nose, maybe a funny way of walking?" McCan said.

"Why, yes. A friend?"

"An acquaintance."

Webster was silent a long time as they walked the street. The appeal of Deadwood was greatly diminished by the trouble with Wyatt and Sturley. Now McCan felt they were merely marking time until the next encounter.

Neither he nor Webster were gunfighters, and they knew it. Wyatt, by high standards, probably was not, either. But his quarrelsome nature and the fact that he routinely carried a pistol indicated he was at least oriented toward violence. McCan wondered if he had ever killed a man.

Night fell and brought out Deadwood's balance of human refuse. They reminded McCan of roaches scurrying from beneath his grandmother's old iron stove as she stoked it at the old Missouri homestead.

He and Webster went into a saloon and crowded the bar. The place was packed; poker games under way all around—an enticement for McCan any other time. Plump saloon girls who looked bad and smelled worse moved about with pitchers of beer and bottles of whiskey. In the corner, a piano player and fiddler pounded and sawed their instruments, each racing the other for the final crescendo.

"Take a look," muttered McCan.

Wyatt and Sturley came through the front door; both were very drunk. Sturley's eyes were sunset red, his hair matted on top and sticking out ridiculously on the sides. Wyatt's face was pasty, his nose puffy. The swelling from his suffered blow of the morning made his eyes squint in the middle of a fist-sized bruise spanning his nose.

"You did a real job on him, Bob," McCan said. "I'd say more than his face is swollen."

"I wish he'd just go off and let it be," Webster said.

"He won't. Well, he just saw us."

Wyatt stared at them. His eyes, made ugly by his bruised face, narrowed and became uglier. His fists clenched, unclenched, the right one near a new Colt in his belt. Sturley tried to look threatening too, but a shadow of fear in his expression spoiled the charade.

"Let's go over to them," Webster said.

"No," McCan said. "If anyone starts trouble, let it be them."

The stare-down went on another minute, neither side moving. Then the saloon door opened, and a drunk came in and stumbled against Sturley. That broke the back-and-forth eyeballing, and Sturley and Wyatt left.

Webster and McCan found a table and sat down. Webster ordered a beer, but as he lifted it to his lips, he stopped and shook his head. "Better steer clear of it tonight," he said.

"Both of us," McCan noted.

Webster said, "There's no reason for you to get any deeper into this. It's my fight."

"Not just yours anymore. They've drawn a bead on me too, just for being your friend."

Webster smiled. "Maybe we ought to work a claim together when this is done."

"I'd thought of that myself. We'll talk it over when we get all this behind us."

The conversation waned. They watched the head of Webster's beer dissolve and go flat. Finally Webster took a breath and said, "Let's get it done."

Together they left the saloon. McCan toyed with the butt of his Colt, fingers sweating. The pistol felt heavy on his leg.

Outside, the street was crowded, all of Deadwood's usual nocturnal action under way. McCan looked around, but did not see Wyatt or Sturley. But they were there—he'd bet on it.

As they passed the door of a brothel, Wyatt and Sturley stepped from an alley and faced them. "We're going to settle it right now, nigger," Wyatt said.

"Move aside," ordered McCan.

Wyatt laughed. "You'll die too."

McCan turned to Sturley. "What about you? Are you brave enough to draw on two armed men?"

Sturley, as usual, looked scared; his courage lived and died based on the momentary fluctuations of temper.

"Let's let 'em be, Jimmy," Sturley said. "I don't feel like killing nobody."

Wyatt saw his chance at battle slipping away. He flung a bitter frown at his partner, paused a moment, then grabbed at his pistol.

He was clumsy, inexperienced as a gunman. That gave McCan and Webster time to leap to either side. Wyatt's first shot plowed the dirt, succeeding only in drawing attention. Men appeared at windows and doorways. A woman screamed. The street around them cleared.

McCan drew and aimed at Wyatt, but the freckled redhead dodged back into the alley. Webster's pistol homed in on Sturley, who ran off wildly into the darkness.

Everything yielded to silence and racing pulses. Webster and McCan were alone. Then someone yelled "Look out!"—and a rapid series of things happened.

A shot roared, and Webster spasmed as if bolt-struck. His pistol fell to his feet, and blood dripped and pooled around it as he swayed. McCan saw Wyatt—he had come around the building and shot Webster in the side.

McCan yelled and swung his pistol around as Wyatt sent two more slugs into Webster's body. McCan fired but missed; Wyatt turned to him as Webster collapsed.

Suddenly, something loomed between McCan and his foe. McCan saw a dirty white shirt stretched over broad shoulders, a head of collar-length gray-black hair, a pair of canvas-clad legs spread in a fighting stance. The man raised a Remington and fired; Wyatt's body kicked back and he was dead, with his pistol smoking in his hand. The tall intruder holstered the Remington and turned and smiled at McCan. It was the man McCan had seen laughing in the saloon doorway earlier in the day.

McCan went to Webster. His brown eyes stared sightlessly skyward.

Another man came to his side. It was Caleb Black. He touched Webster's bloodied chest, felt for a heartbeat, and shook his head.

"He's gone," Black said.

CHAPTER 6

McCan sat in the darkest corner of the darkest saloon he could find and brooded over a beer. A tired-looking undertaker had carted away Webster's corpse an hour before, muttering and cursing the dead man for interrupting his supper. He had eaten later than usual because of a knifing death early in the afternoon. Webster's murder forced him to cut short his time at the table; he took it as a personal imposition.

Though McCan and Webster had not known each other long enough to be truly close friends, McCan had sincerely liked the man. Webster once told McCan he had been born a slave in Alabama, and though freed as a boy, had never really felt like his own man. Mining in the Black Hills had been more to Webster than a chance to make money. It had been his doorway to the most freedom he ever would have known. Wyatt had stolen that from him.

Caleb Black entered the saloon and found McCan. "I'm sorry about your friend," he said. "At least the Wyatt boy got what was due him. But let me tell you something: I recognized the man who shot Wyatt."

"Who?"

Black sat down. "I don't know his name, just his face. He was one of the bandits who robbed me along the Deadwood Trail. I'll find his name, just you wait."

"His name is Evan Bridger." The speaker was Hardin Crowley. He joined them at the table. "Luke, I never went back to the wagons. I got to thinking about you and Webster staying on, and I just couldn't leave. I sent your money for the horses back by Sterling Slater. I heard about Webster. What a shame."

"Tell me about this Evan Bridger," Black said.

"Nothing to tell but his name. I heard it called by somebody who had seen what happened. I've heard Ben Weaver mention him as one of the bandits along the Pierre-Deadwood route."

"I owe him my life, I suppose," McCan said. "If he hadn't cut in, it's even money whether it would be me or Wyatt dead right now."

"I owe him too," Black said in a different tone. "The man tried to murder me on the trail."

McCan saw a change of topic was called·for. "Did you find your brother?"

"I did. He has a place out toward Lead. Just a shack, but on a good claim. I'm welcome there, and that's what counts."

"I wish I was in your shoes," McCan said. "Some hard work is what I need to take my mind off what happened. That, or a good poker game."

"At the moment, I'm mostly interested in Evan Bridger," Black said.

"What are you hinting at?" McCan asked, for some reason beginning to feel irritated.

"It's personal. Not your worry. Suffice it to say you don't harm a Black unless you're ready for the same in return. Eye for an eye—that's in the Bible."

"So is Balaam's jabbering ass," McCan said. He stood and walked out of the saloon.

Hardin Crowley grinned philosophically at Black. "I don't think he means it personal. He's worked up about Webster."

Black unlimbered his long legs beneath the table and wrapped his body across his chair. "I don't really care. I know what I need to do, and I'll do it. Evan Bridger should've never took the first shot at me."

Black didn't show up when they buried Webster. Hardin Crowley and McCan stood by as a hired preacher assured them that the colored brethren do have souls, yes indeed, that Webster was as much a man as any of us, and McCan, never having thought otherwise, merely shrugged and gave the man two dollars. The preacher tucked it into his heavy Bible and walked away, smiling like an aged cherubim.

Crowley left too, and McCan meandered alone about the grave, trying to figure out just what was nagging at him. He wandered over to a spruce grove and sat down, slumping into the shade. He went to sleep, and when he awakened an hour later, he thought he had it figured out.

It was that Sturley had gotten away clean after starting the whole thing. Wyatt might have dominated the dispute at the end, but Sturley had been the catalyst. And so far, he had taken not so much as a fist in the jaw for starting a run-in that had cost a good man his life.

Well, God help him, McCan would make Sturley pay. McCan hefted his Colt and studied it. He looked around for a target, and settled on a pine knot many yards distant. He carefully aimed and fired. The pistol bucked; the knot didn't even spit dust. He fired again,

again, until the chambers were empty. Not a hit.

He reloaded and tried again, and this time a shot connected. The next time was even better. Three slugs shattered the knot.

His ammunition low, McCan holstered the pistol and headed back into Deadwood. *Let Sturley show up now*, he thought. *I'll splinter his head like that pine knot.*

He rode down the center of the street and pretended to search for Sturley. He thought he saw him, and suddenly his last meal was at his throat, threatening an exit. *Better practice some more. Not ready yet.* Then he saw it wasn't Sturley at all, and felt ashamed, like all Deadwood could look through him and see the fear tapeworming through his insides.

The next day he went back to Webster's grave and practiced some more; he improved. He came back the next two days. Each was the same: shoot out more ammunition, gather a bit more skill, a little more confidence, and ride into Deadwood looking for Sturley—but not too hard. Finally he allowed himself to drop the pretense and admit he didn't really want to find Sturley at all. He admitted one thing more: it wasn't Sturley's escape from punishment that ate at him. It was that he himself had been so scared when Wyatt faced him that he probably would have taken a bullet had not Evan Bridger stepped in.

That was why he had come here and fired all those useless shots. It was a waste. He couldn't bring back Webster, nor atone for past fears by becoming a jury-rigged pistoleer well after the fact.

He spat a curse and fired off a quick shot at a blackbird on a pine stump. The bird flew into feathers and red spray, and McCan exclaimed at his accuracy; he hadn't even aimed.

"Now you're getting the hang of it, son," a voice

from behind him said. He wheeled. It was Evan Bridger.

"I been watching you shoot. You got the skill, but you try too hard, overaim. What you have to do is let that pistol become part of your hand. Point it like a finger. You'll hit your target nine times out of ten."

McCan was wordless. He felt strangely awed.

"Let me show you," Bridger said. He drew out his Remington, and five quick shots erupted. Two hundred feet away, a pear-sized rock became dust.

"Point and shoot natural, without the strain," he said. "And always keep one last round in your cylinder. A man who faces a gunfight with empty cylinders is asking to be killed."

McCan found his voice. "Luke McCan's my name," he said. "I want to tell you how grateful I am for what you did back in town." He paused. "Though I'm not sure why you did it."

"I'm not, either," Bridger said. "It seemed the thing to do at the time. I saw the darky buffalo that redtopped fellow in the afternoon, and it was about the funniest thing I ever did see. I guess I took a liking to him, and when old Red-Top shot him, I just jumped in."

"You probably saved my skin," McCan said. He lifted his Colt. "I'm not much good with this thing. I wasn't any good at all when my friend needed me to be."

"You do much shooting in your boyhood, son?"

"Nothing much with a pistol—mostly squirrel hunting. I always was a good marksman with a rifle."

"Loosen up and you'll be a good pistol man too." Bridger smiled, showing even teeth. "Being a good pistol man can be a good thing, or bad. Depends on how a man uses it."

McCan thought back to what had happened to

Caleb Black on the trail, and asked: "How do *you* use it, Mr. Bridger?"

"Any way I please," he said. "I see you know who I am."

"I asked."

Bridger mounted a big black gelding tied to a branch nearby. "I expect I'll see you around some more," he said, and rode away.

McCan suddenly felt a crazy urge to do two contradictory things: to warn Bridger of how Caleb Black had hinted at retribution for the trail attack, and to raise his Colt and put a slug through Bridger's brain. The first urge was the offspring of gratitude; the second came from some deeper source that one day McCan would identify as intuitive foreknowledge, but which now seemed mere insanity.

So he did not shout or shoot. He just watched Bridger ride away.

CHAPTER 7

———

McCan wondered why he remained in Deadwood at all. So far, he had made no attempt to become a miner. He suffered a general malaise, and when his money began running out, eaten up by meals and boarding-house rent, he began playing poker.

He was a good poker player, and Deadwood a good poker town, so he easily made enough money to sustain himself. But he refused to think of himself as a gambler—just as he always had all those previous times the cards had held him—and told himself he would begin mining the next day, or next week, or maybe the week after that. But every night he would sit up with stonefaced men, circling a table, staring at his hand through the smoke of his cigarette. When the gaming was done, he would stagger off to his room— usually several dollars richer—and sleep until midday. Then he would loiter away the afternoons out of town, still practicing with his Colt, but not knowing why. Sturley was a dead issue; the big coward probably had run back to Weaver and the wagon train and Pierre.

Secretly, McCan worried. He felt like a powder keg that might blow, or might just fizzle out. He had gone through something like this right after his parents had been killed, but it hadn't lasted. Webster's murder had brought it all back, though. He thought of writing his sister for advice—but not now. Later. When he was through gambling.

Bound for trouble, bound for crime. Such had been his own mother's prediction for him. He remembered it often now, and didn't deny it like he once had. His mother always had seen the worst in him, even when wanting the best for him. Maybe she was right, he mused. He'd think about it again, after the next poker game.

A rain came and went; McCan walked the muddy street. He stepped across a soaked drunk on the boardwalk, wrinkling his nose at the sewer-pit smell of the town, boosted now to a nearly intolerable level by the rain.

A man across the street caught his eye. He was dark, so much so that McCan first took him for a black man. On closer inspection, the man proved to be an imprecise mongrelization of Spanish and Anglo, with maybe some redskin thrown in. His mustache was wide and so thickly waxed it reflected the sun. His other facial hair was something between a neglected scruff and a true beard. A sombrero pulled low across his grimed forehead enhanced the Spanish look.

Noticeable as the man was, it was the one with him who drew McCan's interest: Caleb Black. Black spoke to the dark man, then glanced around the way men do at the doors of back-street brothels. Black and the man walked into an alley. Sun glinted on the butt of a pistol thrust into the stranger's belt. The man was a gunman. It might as well have been written on him.

* * *

His name was Morgan Hamm. McCan learned it when they brought him in, draped over the back of his horse. He had been shot three times in the chest, but not before being efficiently sliced up by a knife.

"Somebody tortured him bad," said a stranger who watched Hamm's corpse flopping past on the horse's rump. "Whoever did it didn't want him dead too quick."

"Why would they want him dead at all?" McCan asked.

"Hamm's a hired gunman. Kills for pay. Probably whoever did this was supposed to be his victim, but turned the tables. He probably got tortured so he would tell who hired him."

McCan thought about that a moment, then said, "Oh, no."

The stranger gave him an inquiring look. McCan ran for the livery.

Where was Caleb's brother's claim? Out toward Lead, Caleb had said. That was little help, but all he had. McCan had to get there now.

He galloped through the middle of the street, his mount's hooves splashing puddles, his reckless passing evoking a curse from a back-stepping man he nearly ran over. McCan sped past him and out of town.

McCan rode past claims where miners labored. He looked at their faces, but did not know them. They watched him with vague frowns, seeing urgency in his manner.

"Where is Walter Black's place?" he shouted at a trio of them. Two stared back in silence, but the third pointed and said, "Yonder, maybe half a mile. Cut left on the trail through the pines."

McCan spurred his tiring mount. He rounded a bend a quarter-mile ahead, then reined to a halt. A rider came toward him, lazily plodding along.

"Howdy," Evan Bridger said. He touched his hat. "Fine day, Mr. McCan."

McCan watched him round the bend. Then he dug rowels into horseflesh and plunged on, fearing he was too late.

Walter Black's claim was humble, a simple shed with a canvas roof provided his shelter. McCan dismounted in the yard of pounded dirt. Slowly, he approached the open door.

"Hello?"

No response. A bird called and the creek splashed, but that was all.

"Caleb?"

He pushed the door further open and stepped inside. Sunlight spilled in.

A man sat at the table, leaning back against the wall. McCan could scarcely make him out in the shadows.

"Hello? Caleb?"

The man said nothing, did not move. McCan stepped into the shadows himself, and understood why.

This was not Caleb Black. But a strong facial resemblance was there, and McCan knew he had found Walter Black. He had been eating bread with butter and drinking coffee when Bridger came in. The coffee was still steaming.

In Walter Black's forehead was a neat, round bullet hole. A thin trail of blood marked the space between his eyes and spread across his nose. McCan did not want to see more. He turned away, wondering where he would find Caleb's corpse.

He walked to the back of the shed and looked about the clearing, but saw no sign of Caleb.

McCan called Caleb's name and headed toward the woods. He walked through the spruces and pines, and heard a faint but identifiable sound: a man crying.

McCan followed the sound. He found Caleb Black hugging the base of a tree, crying, with his eyes squeezed shut.

"Are you wounded?"

Black shook his head.

"Walter is dead, Caleb."

Black's voice strained: "I know."

"Evan Bridger did it. I saw him riding away. He tortured your hired gunman into telling him you hired him. He probably thought Walter was you."

"I just hid," Black said. "Hid like a coward."

"Come on," McCan said. "We've got a grave to dig."

McCan helped Black to his feet, and together they walked to the clearing.

CHAPTER 8

———

After Walter Black was buried, Caleb Black stayed drunk three days, and on the fourth went looking for Evan Bridger. McCan, who had stayed at the Black claim after the murder, figured he would see Black no more. But only a day later he was back, sober, saying the talk was that Evan Bridger had left the Black Hills. Headed north.

"So what will you do, Caleb?" McCan asked.

Black rubbed his chin and looked around. "Mine this claim, I reckon. And I'd like you to help me. Put away the cards; a man who plays poker gets into trouble, and folks in trouble a lot of times get hurt."

You're a fine one to preach to anybody, McCan thought. But he knew Black was right.

"All right. I'll try it for a few days. But I don't know a thing about mining."

"I'll show you what I know."

That proved to be relatively little. Caleb Black had been at the job only a short time himself; he was nearly as green as McCan. But the work satisfied both of them. McCan ceased his trips to town and the poker tables. He missed the money at the beginning, but with time, their takes increased. McCan thought he had found his calling. He scribed out a letter to his sister in Missouri, telling her the good things that had happened, omitting the tragedies of Bob Webster and Walter Black.

Three months passed. McCan was convinced by then that Caleb Black had gotten over Walter's death. They never discussed it, and he no longer bore the haggard, haunted look that had marked him those first days.

Then, one night, McCan awoke and found Caleb's bunk empty. He went to the door and saw him outside, walking around fast and nervous, pumping his arms up and down like a man about to explode. McCan knew then he had not gotten over the murder at all, maybe never could.

For almost six months they mined and redeemed their gold as usual—every day like the rest. Black still seemed happy, and there were no more restless nights. Then, one night in early spring, he left.

McCan found a note on the door: BRIDGER IN WYOMING—GONE TO FIND HIM. MAY BE BACK SOON OR IT MIGHT BE AWHILE. WHICHEVER, YOU KEEP ON AND THE GOLD IS YOURS. SHALL SEE YOU AGAIN, CALEB.

McCan kept on alone for a week. But without Caleb Black, it was dull work. One night, he slipped on his hat, pocketed his money, and rode into Deadwood. There he found a poker game, made a few dollars. The next night he went back. From then on, his course was set, and mining gradually gave way to poker.

Jack Parker was a big man with smallpox scars, a little talent for poker, and a propensity for big talk. He was new to Deadwood, his background unknown. McCan took a bit of his money over cards nightly for two weeks, but Parker never seemed to mind. He kept his big smile and guffawing laugh, and turned over his losses with unfading good humor.

"I like you, McCan," he said. "You've got a good look about you. The kind of man I like to work with."

"What line are you in?"

"High profits, son, high profits. We'll talk some more about it when the time is right."

McCan dismissed the vague talk and concentrated on his gambling. But then his luck went bad. For three consecutive nights he lost badly at the table. Parker came to him and threw a fleshy arm across his shoulder.

"Take a break from the game tomorrow night," he said. "Head out to the little house beside Tolbert's Gunwright Shop and wait for me. I want to talk something over with you. Business."

McCan would have said no any other time. But his luck was low—*he* was low. He nodded without much thought, and the next night went to the designated place.

The house was two rectangular rooms joined by a hallway; the roof was flat and leaky. McCan entered it. Flies swarmed through an atmosphere thick with the smell of Jack Parker's person, for he lived here. Tonight he waited by a window. When McCan came in, Parker scowled at him.

"You're late," he said.

"I don't even know why I'm here."

"It doesn't matter much now. They went ahead without you. I'd decided you weren't going to show."

McCan waved his hat at the flies. "Explain all this to me, would you?"

But Parker had stopped listening. He straightened

and looked into the dark street. "They're coming!"

"Who?"

Two riders came past the window and cut around the house. Parker rushed to a back door and opened it. McCan recognized two men who sometimes joined the poker games, but who more often loitered in the background, hanging around Parker. They dismounted and walked around to a packhorse they led.

"Did you get it?" Parker asked.

"Take a look," said one of the men. He and the other lifted a pack off the back of the third horse. It was heavy, for both grunted at the effort.

"Get it inside!" Parker said. "Did anybody see you?"

"We were careful."

Inside, they laid the pack on the floor. It made a loud, metallic clump on the floorboards. Parker closed the shutters and threw back the cloth pack cover. Underneath was a small but heavy strongbox.

"Oh, sweet thing, there's no woman finer than you," Parker said. He rubbed his hands together, then fiddled with the lock. "I can saw it off easiest," he said.

"What's going on here?" McCan asked.

"What's it look like?" one of them asked.

"Like robbery."

The man frowned and said to Parker: "Who is this, anyway? Why's he here?"

"He's a latecomer," Parker said. "He's fine. Just not filled in yet."

"I don't want any part of this," McCan said.

"There. See?" the first man said, waving his hand at McCan. "He don't even want to do it. Why you always dragging in extra baggage, Jack?"

Parker didn't answer, for he was working on the lock with a saw. Sweat beaded out on his red face, then began dripping on the strongbox. His well-greased locks swung back and forth across his forehead as he sawed.

"I'm leaving," McCan said. He turned toward the door.

One of the men made as if to draw his pistol, but McCan drew first and thrust his weapon against the man's chin. Just then, there was noise outside—a horse approached, then they heard voices.

"*Law!*" said one of the thieves.

"I thought you weren't followed," Parker said.

McCan holstered his pistol. "That's *law* out there? And me in here with—"

Parker swore. He had thrown open the box. Inside was a handful of change, just a few low-denomination bills.

The men outside came to the door. Parker leaped up, stuffing the money in his pocket. He ran out the back door, and the others followed. McCan was left alone in the house.

"Open this door!" somebody shouted from the front.

McCan almost obeyed, the response automatic. Then he thought again, and ran after the others out the back door.

Thank providence he had tethered his mount in the rear. He leaped astraddle and rode away, hearing yelling behind him as the front door was kicked in and the empty strongbox discovered. A shot popped flatly, and a slug sliced the air high above him. He bent lower and rode as hard as he could until he was out of Deadwood, and knew as he left he could not go back.

A week later, McCan sat by a campfire on the windswept prairie and wrote the following:

Mrs. Martha Hyatt
Independence, Missouri

My Dear Martha,

I'm thinking of you and home tonight because now I've got no home at all. My old partner, Caleb Black—about who I wrote you before—is gone, headed out to find a man who killed his brother, and probably will kill him before he is through, and that is a shame because Caleb is a good man but for his temper and his vengeful ways.

Since he has gone I have not done well, I am sorry to tell you. In your confidence I will be honest—without meaning to I've fallen in with common outlaws, and I guess am not much better than one myself. I listened to a man named Jack Parker and didn't recognize him for a thief and a scoundrel and that is my fault. We are on the run from the law, and all for about fifty dollars in bills and coins.

If you scorn me for this I do not blame you and expect no better. Our mother might have been right about me after all, though you always took my side with her, which I will always be grateful for. Anyway, I am out of Deadwood now and near the Powder River in the Montana Territory, writing this letter by the light of our campfire. I am still with Jack Parker, for I have nobody else to run with and he is at least some protection in the wilderness. There were two others with us, but they cut out and left three days ago.

I don't know what we will do or where we will go. I am sorry also to tell you I've been playing poker a lot more again and may have to keep it up to make some money, though like you always said, it takes a man's worth from him to live on gambled money.

Forgive my gloomy writing, but it makes me feel better to tell of it, even though I know you would want to hear better of me.

Mention me to old friends, but don't tell them what I'm about, nor your family, for I am ashamed of it. Say prayers for me, for I have forgot how and don't think I would be heard in any account. I hope you will hear better from me the next time I write you, and maybe even by the time you receive this my situation will be better, for I am nowhere near a post and cannot send this until I don't know when.

Your foolish but devoted brother,
Luke M.

CHAPTER 9

—

McCan was playing poker in a saloon at Rosebud when he encountered a man he had not expected to see again. He heard a voice, turned, and there he was. For a moment McCan remained frozen, then he thrust his hand to his gun and began to rise.

Parker rose first. "Roy Sturley! Why, I ain't seen you since we gigged frogs together back in Arkansas!"

Sturley smiled at Parker, then saw McCan; the smile vanished. Sturley went chalky white, but McCan, thrown off-balance by Parker's unexpected greeting of Sturley, did nothing. What went through his mind was this: *If I'm so low as to run with a fifty-dollar robber, I might as well go dishonorable all the way and just let Sturley off the hook.*

Feeling the sense of relief that comes with abandoned principles, McCan sank back into his seat and toyed with his cards. Sturley alternated between glancing at McCan with poorly hidden fear and flashing nervous grins at Parker.

After more bubbling about Arkansan boyhood

days—which, McCan gathered, involved an excessive amount of frog-gigging, petty theft, fornication, and arson—Parker turned to McCan and said, "Luke, I want you to meet the finest partner a man ever had. I grew up with this cuss. Roy Sturley, this here is Luke McCan."

Sturley looked as if he would gladly sacrifice a mouthful of teeth to be anywhere else. McCan smelled the fear in him. Without the support of a flared temper or a bellyful of alcohol, Sturley was as meek as he had been when Ben Weaver had knocked him back on the trail to Deadwood.

"We've already had the pleasure," McCan said. "Sturley and me have known each other since we were teamsters together. Right, Roy?"

Sturley nodded.

"Well, who'd a-thought it!" Parker exclaimed. "This is just mighty fine, all of us getting together by accident like this. Roy, sit down and let us deal you in."

"I'm broke," Sturley said.

"Your credit's good with us, Roy—right, Luke?"

"Well, I recall that I owe Roy a little something myself," McCan said. He said it to watch Sturley shudder, which he did.

They played two hours, and McCan won handily. He rarely cheated at cards—though he had the ability—but tonight he did cheat, just to drive Sturley deep into his debt. When the game was done, Sturley was humiliated, McCan satisfied.

The group retired to the prairie for the night. McCan spread his bedroll and lay down, but sleep eluded him. Through his mind played the scene of Bob Webster's death, and his own obsession shortly thereafter of making Sturley pay for his role in that injustice.

By the next morning, a new memory was lodged in McCan's brain: a memory of how he had risen in the dark after seeing Sturley do the same. Sturley had quietly taken his horse and crept off; McCan had followed. Out on the open land he had cut Sturley off, made him stop.

"I decided earlier I would forgive you for what you did," he told the frightened man. "Then I thought about it, and changed my mind."

McCan raised his pistol. "For Bob," he said as he squeezed the trigger.

McCan recalled it all with clarity—unusual for him, for he usually did not remember his dreams. Only one part had really happened: Sturley had, indeed, slipped away. McCan had not seen it, for sleep had finally come, bringing with it the dream of revenge McCan could never really have performed, but which gave a certain satisfaction nonetheless.

Parker was saddened and mystified by Sturley's nocturnal departure. "I can't figure it out," he said. "Why would he do it?"

"I guess we'll never know," McCan said.

"Well, he'll miss out on a good deal," Parker said. "We're heading for the Missouri Breaks, son. Good money to be made up that way."

"How so?"

"Rustling, my friend, rustling."

McCan immediately saw a clear image of himself swinging a couple of feet above the ground, neck stretched out nearly a foot long, head slumped to the side, eyes half shut, and tongue dangling out. It was enough to empty his stomach, but he only smiled and said, "Sounds mighty good to me."

From that moment on he looked for a chance to leave. None arose for a long time, not until days later, when they reached the Breaks and rode to an old cattle station occupied by a coal-dirty Irishman named Todd Feeney. Feeney knew Parker, and welcomed him, but watched McCan warily.

McCan spent one night there, and the next day; when darkness fell again, he took his horse and rode fifteen miles through the night. He camped in a draw at the bend of the Missouri, slept half the next day, and waited out the rest. Just before sunset he rode again.

Satisfied he had not been followed, he relaxed, let a deep breath of relief flow out like a prayer, and put his days of criminal association forever behind him. Then he cut southward and rode toward the little settlement of Glendive, having no plan, no goal, and very little money.

PART II

THE TIMBER CREEK CATTLE ENTERPRISE

CHAPTER 10

In Glendive, McCan found a job as a clerk in a general store. He passed a spring and summer in relative comfort, but in the fall and winter, business grew lean. Cattlemen who came in complained of wolves and rustlers, and bought mostly on credit. The next spring the store closed when the owner abruptly decided to head back east.

McCan turned to the cattle industry. He found a job on a ranch near the Tongue River and learned the requisite skills from a one-toothed old Texan named Rufus Meuller. In the fall, he went on his first roundup.

That was a harder venture than being a teamster, and about equal to mining. He slept five or six hours at night—sometimes in the rain—and spent what seemed ten times that many in the saddle. On roundup, his standard meal was a concoction of lean beef, cattle heart, brains, guts, and hot sauce, all cooked together under the name son-of-a-bitch stew. "Eat it with gratitude, boy," Meuller would say. "Not only will it fill your belly, but it'll keep you dewormed."

After the roundup, he spent a winter in a line camp on Mizpah Creek, bored and reading the backs of soup cans to remain sane. His job was to keep the cattle of his home ranch within that spread's accepted range, and he did the task well, despite no cooperation from weather or cattle.

When spring came he moved on, looking for a larger spread. He bought a weary old horse and a good saddle and rode to the Timber Creek Cattle Enterprise near the Mountain Sheep Bluffs, about fifty miles west of Glendive and the same distance north of Milestown. There he sought out the ranch boss, Abe Hunt, and asked for work.

There were others there at the same time, also seeking jobs, and a dozen of them lined up in the shade of a lean-to, awaiting the verdict. Hunt would have made the decision alone and quickly under normal circumstances, but today a representative of the holding company that owned the ranch was present and wanted a hand in the hiring.

The company rep's name was Henry Sandy; he looked like a Bostonian and talked like an Iowan. He chose McCan and five others; Hunt sealed the choices with a nod. The new employees headed to the bunkhouse to deposit their possessions, but Hunt motioned McCan aside first.

"That horse of yours ain't worth poleaxing," he said. "Pack it in the corral and pick out a good one. We'll fill out the rest of your string later."

"He likes the look of you, neighbor," said a man at the corral. "He always gives first pick to them he likes."

McCan went to the bunkhouse. It smelled almost fishy from sweat, and McCan was further disheartened to see a grizzly of a man pick a louse from his beard and throw it to the dirt floor. McCan jumped and almost yelled when the man suddenly produced a pistol from beneath his blanket and shot the evicted parasite.

"A big one," the man said.

McCan drew his Colt and pumped two more slugs into the floor at the man's feet. "Sure was," he said. "You just winged it."

After dumping his goods, he walked out the door. At least three men had witnessed the incident. McCan figured he had just saved himself a lot of harrassment; the story would spread ranch-wide by nightfall, and the Timber Creek crew would know he was no greenhorn ripe for torment.

It was mid-April, and the plains turned green after the long winter. Snows on the western mountains' lower slopes melted, making rivers and creeks rise. The barrens became active again.

Out of the hidden valleys and ravines where they had passed the winter, cattle emerged to feed on the new grass. It soon would be time for the spring roundup, when the losses of the winter would be assessed, and new calves branded.

McCan was given the job of preparing the chuck wagon for roundup. Helping him was Stewart Biggs, the lice-shooter from the bunkhouse. Together they greased the wheels and axles and replaced a damaged sideboard. They cleaned mouse nests from the chuck box and strung a new tarpaulin beneath the wagon as a pocket for wood and chips. They worked under the guidance of John Weatherby, the Timber Creek cook— maker of the Montana Territory's finest raisin pudding.

As McCan expected, the louse story earned him respect. Biggs and Weatherby both seemed fond of McCan, and he was popular among the crew at large. A particular friend was Dan Tackett, nearly twenty years McCan's senior, and an old man among cowboys. Tackett had come up from Texas with the first Montana herds, and had worked ranches from Dakota to the Deer Lodge Valley. McCan learned that Tackett had once been married, and had lost a son to the Cheyenne—a boy who, Hunt told McCan, looked a lot like him, something McCan took as a partial explanation for Tackett's attachment.

Two days into May, the Timber Creek punchers rode into Milestown to begin the roundup. With them went punchers and reps from scores of other spreads over eastern Montana and western Dakota, even some from northern Wyoming. Cattle ranged far on the open land, despite efforts to contain them, and it was common to see reps from far-spread ranches in the roundup.

McCan rode beside Tackett as they slowly approached Milestown. The town looked sleepy and drab across the distance, but that was a mirage, conjured from the mist of the nearby Yellowstone. Milestown was no Deadwood, but it was a lively enough place, particularly when cowboys were in town.

Tackett bit off a chew of tobacco and settled it into his jaw, then lit a cigar. He was the most tobacco-permeated man McCan knew, seldom going to sleep without an unlit cheroot between his lips. "You're going to snore that thing down your gullet," Hunt would warn him repeatedly. But Tackett never did.

Tackett gestured toward the panorama of men, horses, and wagons.

"You'll see good times here today, Luke," he said. "Folks getting together after a long time apart like to whoop it up a little. I wonder if old Stanley Branch is here? He's with the Connors crew down on the Powder, I ain't seen him since last year."

Tackett was excited, and it rubbed off on McCan, for Tackett was not prone to easy enthusiasm. But today his eyes laughed and his shoulders were thrown back.

McCan dismounted at the circus of cowboys. It seemed all of them were talking, laughing, and cussing at the same time. To the right, five men played poker, the pot being pay the players would not receive until roundup was done. Elsewhere, a footrace was in progress, and beyond that, a horse race. Two men arm wrestled at McCan's left, and nearby, others huddled around a bottle, passed in violation of roundup rules. On the fringe of the group, someone with a harsh and supervisory expression tried to shoo off a wagon of prostitutes who had come over from the far side of town to advertise their inventory.

McCan wandered through the crowd, occasionally nodding at those he knew from previous ranch work. At length he saw a rope corral, in which a husky black man carefully approached a horse with a wild eye. Unlike the rest, the men at the corral were silent as gravediggers.

The man slowly twirled a rawhide rope as he eased up to the defiantly snorting horse. He was like a cat, moving silently, loop always twirling, until at last he cast it true over the horse's neck.

The animal contorted, reared, kicked, jerked its head to free itself. Two men moved in to help the buster keep hold of the rope, and finally looped it around a snubbing post set deep in the earth.

The horse braced and pulled until he threw himself over, and in a second the buster was on the animal, hobbling it with the rope now jerked free from the post. He whipped a bridle from his belt and secured it in place.

He let the horse up again, then approached with the blanket and saddle. After several tries, fifty pounds of leather and metal were cinched on the horse. Before the horse could respond, the buster twisted its ear enough to hurt and swung into the saddle.

The horse became an explosion of hide, dust, and lather. The buster was thrown high and hard, one arm flapping like a wing. As the horse tried to throw him, the men at the corral broke their silence: "Ride that thing, Bill!" "Don't let him throw you, son!"

On it went for several minutes, until the weary horse gave up. The buster dismounted, then mounted again, over and over until the horse was accustomed to the feel of it.

The man removed the saddle and bridle and gave the horse a rest. It wasn't fully broken, but its spirit was. Before long, it would be a good working horse.

Dusting off his gray breeches, the buster walked to the side of the corral. Appreciative pats drummed the sweat-ringed shoulders of his blue shirt.

McCan found him later, sipping coffee beside one of the chuck wagons. "You did a fine job on that bronc," McCan said.

"Thanks," the buster said. He looked up, and McCan drew in his breath.

Bob Webster!

"You all right, friend?"

"I don't know what to say—you're the image of a friend of mine who—I lost down in the Black Hills."

The man grew serious. "You knew Bob?"

"Bob Webster—right."

"He was my brother. I'm Bill Webster from the Lazy Arrow."

McCan smiled and stuck out his hand. "I'm proud

to meet you, Bill. I heard Bob speak of you. My name's Luke McCan."

This time it was Bill Webster who looked surprised. "McCan? You were with Bob when he died?"

"Yes, but how . . ."

"*He* told me." The black man pointed at an approaching figure. It was Hardin Crowley. McCan and Crowley saw each other at the same time—Crowley speeded to a near run, his hand already extended.

"Luke! Never figured to see you turn cowboy!"

"What about you, Hardin? I thought you'd still be in Deadwood, getting rich."

"Left two years ago. I see you done met Bill."

"Yeah. Thought I was seeing Bob's ghost for a second, Hardin, you haven't changed. But the times have, that's for sure. You're the first old face I've seen in quite a spell."

They talked several minutes, and Crowley said, "I saw your old partner awhile back, down in Bozeman."

"Caleb?"

"Yeah, but you'd hardly know him. All beard and grit and muscle. He's had a hard road to follow."

"What's he doing now?"

"What do you think? He's trailing Evan Bridger. And it's making him and Bridger both a little famous. There's a magazine back east that wrote about them. Called Bridger the badman with the ghost at his heels, the haunt that won't let him rest. Would you ever have thought such as that out of Caleb, huh?"

CHAPTER 11

—————

After the first week on roundup, McCan quit counting the days. All was repetition, so there seemed no point in keeping up. Only the terrain varied.

Most days McCan worked closely with Dan Tackett, particularly when they entered the land around the Yellowstone. They worked hills and gullies, driving out calves with mothers bawling at their tails, rumbling down to the day herd that followed the chuck and bed wagons and the remuda.

Bill Webster, to McCan's pleasure, was rep on the same roundup team as he. They had little time to talk, but McCan enjoyed the company, for it was much like having Bob Webster back again.

The roundup team of which they were a part split two days into the roundup, one portion heading east, their own smaller one combing the west. They generally followed the contours of North Sunday Creek, moving across the Little Dry, over Crow Rock Creek and up Timber Creek, delving finally into the rugged lands near the Missouri. Here they were not far from

Wolf Point, and the area McCan had reached with Jack Parker.

They worked back along Crow Rock Creek through a series of knolls and gulches. Tackett and McCan had the worst of it today—following a narrow rivulet winding through hills, Tackett low and McCan high on the ridges, where he could scan coulees for strays. They did well, rousting out cattle like rabbits from a bush, and Tackett herded at least twenty before him now.

McCan saw the remuda and the wagons far out on the plains, the day herd spread peacefully beyond it. A thin cloud of dust showed him where some other cowboy was drawing together quite a herd of his own.

McCan galloped to the top of a ridge and looked down as Tackett rounded a bluff and entered a small, lush valley where several cattle grazed. Tackett waved up to indicate he saw them, and McCan sent his mount half-sliding, half-walking down the slope to him. An avalanche of gravel rolled ahead.

"Look at this," Tackett said.

They dismounted and walked to the little valley's gaplike mouth. The valley was really a box canyon, and across the entrance was a thin strand of barbed wire. McCan understood what it meant.

His eyes swept the little valley, and he pointed. "Look there. There's been a camp here awfully recent."

"Yep. And I'll bet if you check them cattle every one will have a brand that ain't on the record books yet. This is a running iron operation. Rustle mavericks, brand the yearlings, rebrand the others, hold them until you can register the brand, and have your own herd free and clear, nobody the wiser."

"Guess we ought to tell Abe," McCan said.

"Don't cut the fence or nothing," Tackett said.

"Abe will want to see this as it is." He shook his head. "Damn Missouri River's lined with thieves."

"I know," McCan said. "I was up there a little while."

Tackett looked at him with more interest than his old poker face had shown before, but he said nothing.

When they got back to the camp, Abe Hunt had not come in. They drank Arbuckle coffee and waited for him. When he arrived and heard their story, he looked disgusted, but not surprised. After a quick meal he rode with them to the valley.

Hunt clipped the barbed wire with cutters from his saddlebag. McCan wondered how many ranch and homestead fences had yielded to that tool, for Hunt was a wire-hating man.

The cattle spooked, but the men caught three yearlings. Hunt inspected the new brands on them.

"Running iron, no question," he said. "I've seen no brand like this one before."

"Think we'll find whoever did this?" McCan asked.

"I doubt it," Hunt answered. "They've probably cleared out for the Breaks."

But the next day, Tackett flushed from a coulee a couple of mavericks, a five-foot rattler, and a very scared man. Tackett brought the man into camp. The fellow claimed to be suffering from a blow to the head given to him by an unnamed partner, who had since ridden away.

Hunt watched the man with a grim, ominous expression. "Who are you?"

"My name is Terrence Brown. I'm from the XIT—at least, until a month ago, when I had to take off."

"Why'd you do that?"

"My old mammy took sick, and I had to get her to a doctor in Milestown. But she died."

"Why you out here alone?"

"I was on my way to Rosebud with a man named Ernest Smith. We had jobs lined up there. My horse hit a hole and snapped its leg and I had to shoot it. Then he just popped me with his gun butt and left me, Smith did. I don't know why."

"You say you worked for the XIT?"

"That's right."

"Until a month ago?"

Now Brown looked cautious. "Yes."

Hunt called to one of the men back at the chuck wagon, "Dillard! Come up here." A gangly fellow rubber-legged it over to him.

"Mr. Brown, Dillard here worked the XIT not three months back. He knows every man on the place. Dillard, do you know this man?"

"Never seen him before," Dillard said.

Brown looked scared.

"*I've* seen him," said someone behind McCan. It was Lester Tracey, a young man just shy of twenty. "I can't give all the details, but I was with a bunch of cattlemen who cleaned out a nest of cattle thieves here a few months back, and this here's one that slithered out."

Brown's eyes darted like those of a cornered cur. "If I'm being accused of a crime, I want a fair trial. A courtroom, with a real judge."

"We've got no need for such," Hunt said. He looked around. "That cottonwood should serve the purpose."

Someone found a rope and knotted it into a hangman's noose. As Brown watched in horror, Tackett threw the rope over the branch of the cottonwood.

Brown ran. Tackett stepped out, bounded in broad strides, and took him by the collar. Brown went down, and Tackett dropped his knee onto his belly, full-weight.

They dragged Brown, kicking and yelling, to the cottonwood, where they stood him atop a keg from the chuck wagon and tightened the noose around his neck. McCan's pulse raced as he watched; he was glad he had left the company of Jack Parker.

They pulled the rope tight. "I'm sorry there's not enough drop for a proper slack," Hunt said. "We'll just have to let you choke it out. Do you want a prayer from anyone?"

Brown only glared at him. Hunt shrugged. "Whatever you prefer. Good-bye, thief." He kicked away the stool.

Brown choked, his face red, eyes bulging, horrible sounds coming from inside him. McCan was about to turn away when Hunt drew his pistol and shot the rope in two. Brown dropped to the ground on his rump.

Hunt holstered his pistol. "I spared you because I'm a man who can hardly stand to kill a rattler, not because you deserve to live. Now I want something from you in return. You go to every rustler you know and tell them the territory is full of cattlemen who are about to go to war, and there'll be no mercy shown like you've gotten here. Tell them you were lucky, and the next man won't be. Go. Get out of here."

Brown worked himself to his feet. Hunt drew his knife and cut off most of the rope that trailed down his back. But he left the noose on his neck, and he used the cut-off rope to tie Brown's hands behind his back.

"You can't send me out like this!"

"Start walking."

"But there's no telling what will happen to me!".

"All right, then we can go ahead and hang you."

Brown cursed, but started walking. Tackett drew his pistol and put a slug into the dirt at his heel, and Brown ran.

CHAPTER 12

———

Among cowboys, Jonas Carrington was exceptional in two ways: he had a family—though only a daughter, for his wife was dead—and he had his own house, away from the ranch.

It was the latter distinction that was the most unusual, for several of the Timber Creek hands either had been married at one time or had fathered children without the formality of marriage. Several had kept company with squaws, primarily the handful who had come to Montana in the days of the Alder Gulch mining rush.

Carrington was employed by the Timber Creek Cattle Enterprise, but he worked irregularly, mostly during roundups. The rest of the time he spent raising sustenance crops for himself and his daughter, and that made him an exception in a third way: most cowboys hated any form of sodbusting and refused to do it. Carrington kept busy at it, and he also repaired wagons and did some occasional blacksmithing work.

His daughter, two decades old, was a dark-haired

beauty whose picture Carrington kept in a pillbox in his pocket. Like her father, she was a busy person. She taught piano lessons to the daughters of other ranchers, sometimes to cowboys who used the lessons as an excuse to be close to her. With relatively few women on the plains, the cowboys idolized Jonas Carrington's daughter, though few knew her personally. Jonas, it was rumored, was prone to run off at gunpoint any who came calling without meeting his approval first.

Carrington was shy and quiet by nature, but throughout the roundup had been even more reticent than usual. He stayed alone most of the time, and appeared thoughtful and somewhat troubled.

Near the end of the roundup, Carrington approached Abe Hunt.

"I've got to go home, Abe," he said.

"We will go, in about a week."

"Something's wrong back there. I've got a feeling. I have to go back now."

Abe Hunt pursed his lips, then nodded. "All right. Head on back and do what you need to. Come back here if there's time, and if not, I'll see you back at Timber Creek."

Carrington smiled, thin-lipped and tight. His face looked drawn. "Thank you, Abe." He walked away, rubbing his left arm as if it hurt.

The next morning, Hunt shook McCan awake just before dawn. Weatherby was putting on coffee to boil. Almost everyone else still slept.

"I want you to ride back home with Jonas," Hunt said. "I don't think everything is all right with him."

McCan rubbed his eyes, then nodded. "Whatever you want, Abe. Why's he going back?"

Hunt filled him in. "He's not too happy to have you along. He thinks I'm nursemaiding him."

Carrington was by the chuck wagon, wolfing day-old beans in a rush, too hurried to wait for breakfast. McCan did the same, figuring from Carrington's manner that they might not stop for food the rest of the day. He had barely filled his belly when it was time to go.

Each took an extra mount trailing behind. They rode southeast. When they were about a mile from camp, dawn broke, sending their shadows westward, so long they faded into the horizon.

Carrington said little to McCan. When he did speak, he wasn't unfriendly, but preoccupied. McCan did not ask what Carrington thought was wrong; indeed, he suspected Carrington himself did not know.

They rode until their mounts were lathered and puffing, then paused to give them rest. McCan ate some jerky from his saddlebag; Carrington refused it. They changed mounts and rode on.

McCan noticed Carrington favored his left arm, holding it awkwardly as he rode. McCan asked him about it.

"It's nothing. I strained it a couple of days ago throwing a calf."

In early afternoon, clouds rolled up over the hills, fed by the Missouri River waters many miles to the north. The clouds gathered in a black layer, spread across the sky. A moist wind arose, cool and tingling, and a rumble of thunder came from somewhere deep in the sky and rolled into silence.

Carrington and McCan dug ponchos from their packs and slipped them on. A minute later the clouds put forth drenching splatters too big to be raindrops, too small to be bucketloads. It was like riding ten feet too close to a waterfall. The horses pulled back their ears and trudged, heads down, as lightning slashed above. McCan's poncho turned away all the water it could, then gave up and let it pour through. Carrington said something about hoping the storm didn't stampede the cattle back at the roundup. Yet when a lightning bolt splintered a tree not a quarter-mile away, he didn't seem to notice.

Thunder made Carrington's spare horse skittish, and it pulled away. It ran into the murk, and they saw it no more. Carrington muttered something, but did not go after it.

After an hour the storm slowed into a steady, calmer rain. McCan was chilled and saddleweary, but on they plodded. At sunset the clouds opened, and red light streamed like blood through the gash.

Carrington rode to the top of a slope and halted. He rubbed his left arm again. McCan stopped beside him. Below lay a small cabin beside a creek that gushed rainwater. A light winked on in the cabin window and spilled out around the edges of the shutters.

"Everything looks fine, Jonas," McCan said.

Carrington clicked his tongue and dug rowels into his mount; the exhausted horse moved down the slope. McCan followed.

"She's cooking supper, I bet," McCan said. "I'd say she's a fine cook, huh?"

Carrington, still silent, dismounted about a hundred feet from the house.

"Maggie!" he called.

No answer came. Suddenly it was as if somebody had slipped a shard of ice down McCan's shirt. Carrington's apprehensions became his own, and he reached for his pistol as he dismounted.

"Maggie!"

Still no answer. Carrington drew his pistol and went to the door. With a kick he shattered the latch and the door burst open, revealing a dimly lighted room. In one corner stood Maggie Carrington, pale and scared. About ten feet from her was the rustler Terrence Brown, holding a rifle. He aimed it at Carrington. Brown's hands trembled. Rope burns were starkly visible on his neck. He fired; a slug sang past Carrington and McCan. Carrington moved to the center of the doorway, silhouetted against the light of the room. His pistol thundered and flashed orange fire.

Brown screamed and grasped his chest; the rifle clattered to the floor. Carrington fired twice more, filling the cabin with smoke and sound. When the shooting ended, McCan heard Maggie Carrington's screams.

Brown was dead, three wounds in his chest. Carrington walked to Brown's body, looked at it, then groped at his heart and slid slowly to the floor. He took one shuddering breath and died.

CHAPTER 13

It was his heart that killed him—Brown's shot hadn't even come close. But when news of Jonas Carrington's death got out, he was thought as much a victim of a cattle rustler as if he had been shot by Terrence Brown, rather than merely startled to death by him.

McCan and a neighboring rancher named Oren Marby buried Carrington. Marby, whose left leg was arthritic, stayed home during roundup. Despite his affliction, he dug with gusto when it was time to bury Terrence Brown. He and McCan scraped out a shallow hole, dumped the rustler's body in facedown, and then Marby spat on the corpse as McCan threw in dirt.

In the meantime, Marby's wife took in Maggie, who had become hysterical for only a few moments after her father's death. Then she had pulled herself upright, forced tears away from her eyes, and stilled the trembling of her lips. She rode beside McCan on Carrington's old buckboard, never crying, never speaking.

McCan slept a few hours before starting back to the

roundup. There, news of Carrington's passing was taken badly, particularly by Hunt, who blamed himself for not snuffing out Brown when he had the chance. When the roundup was done and the Timber Creek punchers were home again, several of them secretly sought out Brown's grave and, under the leadership of Stewart Biggs, performed some atrocities on the corpse. It was a useless bit of barbarity, but the only outlet for their rage, and no one complained.

McCan rode to the Marby spread to check on Maggie and found she had gone back home. The girl had vowed to live at her own place, regardless of the bad memories and the loneliness. That made McCan respect her; she was a young lady with grit.

He rode to her house and found her at the well. She was a pretty lady, there was no denying. Much more so even than the pillbox photograph showed. Slender, of medium height, her face oval and dusted with freckles, her shape utterly feminine—she looked like ladies McCan had seen in portraits in fancy parlors back in St. Louis.

He greeted her, and she smiled in return. "I wanted to see if you were making it all right," he said.

"You're kind. And I am all right."

"I was surprised to hear you came back here so fast."

"I've never run from memories, even bad ones," she said. "Mr. McCan, I owe you thanks for the help you were to me. I should have thanked you earlier, but the time wasn't right for saying anything. You understand."

"Of course." McCan looked at the cabin. He noticed a torn muslin window, flapping in the wind.

"While I'm here, I might as well help you out some more, if you'd not mind."

She didn't, so he repaired the window, restoring the

waxed muslin. They talked quietly as he worked. When he was done, he said good-bye and rode away.

When he was out of view, he reached into his pocket and pulled out Jonas Carrington's pillbox. He flipped it open and looked at the picture.

He shouldn't have done it—picking a dead man's pocket. But he wasn't sorry. He pocketed the box and spurred his horse across the prairie.

About a week later, McCan and Abe Hunt sat with coffee cups in hand and tobacco in their jaws.

"I hear you spent some time along the Missouri before you came to us," Hunt said.

"That's right."

Hunt took a slow swallow of coffee before he spoke cautiously. "No offense to you, but that's surely the haunt of thieves."

"No offense taken. That's true. It's why I left."

"You were running with somebody up there?"

"Wasn't there long enough to really run with them. But I kept company with one particular fellow for awhile before he started talking cattle rustling."

Another sip of coffee, another cautious, exploratory question from Hunt: "Are you a man who objects to naming names? 'Cause if you are, it don't . . ."

"Jack Parker. I got no reason to keep his name secret."

Hunt nodded. "I've heard of him. And a Feeney?"

"I met him."

"What about a father and two boys, last name of Bain?"

"Them I don't know."

Hunt nodded. He asked no more questions. But he did say: "Rustling problems are getting worse. Roundup showed it this year, and the winter isn't the only cause. Horses are dissappearing too. Some of the ranchers are hiring range detectives and forming protective associations. There's been a lynching or two, but it doesn't seem to stop the problem."

"You think things are going to get more . . . drastic?"

"I do."

In the days that followed, McCan returned more frequently to Maggie's home. He would work, they would talk. She began fixing some of his meals. McCan thought of her constantly; he spent a lot of time looking at the pillbox portrait.

In September the Marby ranch hosted a dance, and McCan escorted Maggie to it. It was their first public appearance together, and it led to an association between them in the eyes of the locals.

But their involvement remained quiet, mostly private. And it remained, to McCan's disturbance, rather cool. McCan always was aware of something in Maggie's eyes, in the tightness of her shoulders, that kept her a little distant from him. He worried about it, laid awake about it, but said nothing.

The unseen barrier was there when he left for fall roundup, and there when he returned.

Hunt assigned McCan to line-camp duty, and he knew he probably would see Maggie not at all through the winter. The thought was a dull cramp inside him that did not go away, even when Maggie gave him a sack of books as a defense against the inevitable boredom of the lonely winter camp. She was a cowboy's daughter; she understood.

She waved at him until he was out of view across a distant hill, riding toward the line camp with the bag of books slung over his saddlehorn.

CHAPTER 14

———

The snow hit quickly and hard.

McCan got the first hint while trying to determine if a steer that had fallen into a ravine was slightly or seriously injured. There was a sudden, subtle change in the atmosphere, and he anticipated snow by morning.

The steer was badly hurt, so he shot it. He carved out what meat he could handle and went back to the line camp, a low-roofed building of unbarked logs, a small woodshed behind, and a large lean-to shelter for the horses in bad weather. Beside the shelter was a corral fenced with cut saplings.

McCan reached the camp as the first flakes fell. He slung most of the meat into a sack hung from a jutting roof beam, counting on the cold weather to retard spoilage. He went inside and stirred the fire, then greased a skillet for a steak.

He missed Maggie terribly. The first days had been the worst. Now he was more used to the misery, the way a man with a bad back learns to ignore how badly he is hurting.

That night a blizzard came with awesome fury. Wind whistled around the cabin; hard-frozen snow drove against the shutters with a haillike rattle. Every crack in the chinking spewed cold air. McCan huddled beneath a buffalo robe and drank coffee.

He heard a noise outside. One of the horses? When he heard it again, he stood. It *was* a horse, but not one of his own. He had learned to distinguish their whinnies and trumpets from all others, for he heard them constantly through the wall.

McCan checked his pistol and slipped it into the waist of his trousers. He went to the window and partially opened a shutter. Biting wind struck him, and snow whipped in. Squinting against it, he peered out.

The darkness was heavy as a sodden blanket. He could see only six feet, and there was nothing out there but darkness and snow. Then he heard the neighing of a horse again, not more than a few yards away.

"Hello, the camp!"

The wind distorted and weakened the voice. McCan flung the shutter wide and shouted, "I hear you! Ride in!"

He wrapped the buffalo hide tightly around his shoulders and put on his hat. He threw open the heavy slab door and went out. Immediately, snow encrusted his brows and whiskers.

The rider approached on a horse that appeared ready to drop. Huddled in the saddle, the man looked like he was carved from an ice block; long icicles hung from his hat, and his eyes were frozen nearly shut.

He slumped from the saddle as McCan reached him. McCan struggled inside with him and put him on his grass tick bed. He threw a blanket over the man, then went outside and took the horse into shelter. He fed it hurriedly, then went back inside the cabin. He threw off his buffalo robe. In contrast to the bitterness outside, the cabin seemed warm and life-giving.

McCan knelt beside the pale man. He touched him; he felt like a corpse fresh from a mortician's ice room.

McCan took the right hand and slowly began rubbing the blue fingers, warming them, working out the stiffness. He warmed the left hand too, then the toes. The toes worried him. They were badly frostbitten; gangrene could set in.

But to his surprise, the toes warmed beneath his fingers. He felt the throb of a pulse, and glanced up at the face. Color was returning as the ice melted from whiskers and hair. The man breathed steadily, shallow gulps making his chest heave.

McCan worked his way up the arms. The man's breathing deepened; he was asleep. McCan looked again at the face, and pulled back as if a gun had fired near his ear.

Caleb Black!

He was bearded, much more weathered than before. The nearly five years that had passed since last he had seen him had left deep tracks, but this was, indeed, Caleb Black.

McCan pulled the blankets tighter around Black and put the buffalo hide on top of those. He went to the stove and rebuilt the fire, then drank some more coffee as he watched Caleb sleep.

An hour later, Black stirred. He moaned like a hung over man waking up; his eyes opened and he stared at the ceiling.

"How's it feel to be froze, Caleb?" McCan said.

Black's head turned slowly toward him, as if his joints needed oiling. He squinted. McCan raised his coffee cup in salute. Black tried to smile, but couldn't. He did manage a weak, ironic laugh. In a coarse whisper, he said, "I thought for a minute I was back in Deadwood."

"You might have suspected this was the heavenly gates, considering how froze up you got yourself."

"I got lost out there. I was on my way to Miles-town."

"You're a long way from it. And why did you come this way?"

"Give me some coffee and I'll tell you."

McCan gave him a cupful, and also cooked some thin slices of beef. Black ate and drank slowly, taking careful swallows that made him wince.

"I hear you still trail Evan Bridger," McCan said. "Is that why you're in these parts?"

"It is. But I came out here to find you. I heard you worked the Timber Creek spread, so while I was in the area, I had to look you up. They warned me about the snow—I should have listened."

"I can't believe you still chase Bridger. You can't bring back Walter."

"It's not just Walter anymore." Black's eyes turned brooding. "I got married, Luke. Annie was her name. And Bridger killed her—killed *them*, for she had a baby in her."

There was a long silence. "I don't know what to say, Caleb," McCan said.

"I met her over near Virginia City," Black said. "I had been chasing Bridger here and there, finding trails and losing them and finding them again. We had met up a few times, took shots at each other. Sometimes he trailed me, trying to kill me to get me off his back. Finally he got away from me, and I traced him to Virginia City. I never found him, but when I met Annie, Bridger didn't seem to matter anymore. I fell hard, Luke. You ever had a thing like that happen to you?"

McCan smiled, rather sadly, and nodded, but Black wasn't looking. He went on. "I married her and we settled down to start a family. I did this and that to

keep us alive—hunting, trapping, trading, whatever—
and we weren't rich by a long shot, but we were
happy. I all but forgot about Bridger.

"But he didn't forget me. He showed up one night
while I was gone, and he shot Annie. Shot her dead,
right there in our own home, and left a note pinned
to her body, telling me the things he had done before
he . . ." Black couldn't finish. His throat tightened,
squeezing off the words.

"Damn, Caleb," McCan whispered. "I had no idea
he had put you through that."

"It's what he put *her* through that eats at me. I
swear, Luke, I'll be on his trail until one of us is dead,
and if he kills me and it's possible to come back, I'll
be on his trail then too."

McCan nodded. "I understand." He rose and re-
filled Black's cup. "How long will you wait?"

"I'll leave as soon as the snow lets me."

The next morning a foot and a half of snow was
piled out across the prairie. Drifts were saddlehorn-
high in places.

Black waited out the day and one more night, and
then was ready to go. "I'll see you again, Luke," he
said.

McCan nodded. He watched Black ride away until
he was a spot on the field of white. "Caleb!" he yelled.

Black stopped and turned in the saddle.

"You get him—hear?"

Black nodded and waved, then turned away and disappeared into the vast whiteness.

That night it snowed again, hard as before. McCan
prayed for Black, wondering if the heavens heard
prayers for a man who lived for the death of another,
even one as evil as Evan Bridger.

For another day terrible cold lingered, spread like
ice out across the plains. It was weather to freeze a

man's fingers to the reins before dropping his horse from beneath him. There was no way, McCan feared, Black could have made it.

But the next day the cold broke. A period of unusual warmth melted the snow down to the dirt, leaving only patches in shaded recesses, piled up against the north side of rocks and trees and the line-camp cabin.

On a bright Tuesday morning during that lull, Dan Tackett, Abe Hunt, and a blond man McCan didn't know rode out to the camp.

CHAPTER 15

The stranger's name was Jephthah Avery—"Call me
Jeff"—and until recently he had been a woodhawk
along the Missouri, supplying wood to fuel the steam-
boats. Now he was a range detective.

Hunt, as usual, took the lead, and with few prelim-
inaries explained why the group had come.

"All over the territory, cattlemen are responding to
rustling," he said. "But things just keep getting worse.
There's no sign they will improve if we let things go
as they have.

"Back years ago, the worst kind of scum was running loose in Virginia City and Bannack, and it took
outright vigilante activity to take care of them. We're
hoping to stop short of doing all that those regulators
did, and our aim is to be peaceful and law-abiding—
but it's obvious we need to increase our aggression
against the thieves who are robbing us blind.

"This spring, a group of us will ride north to the
Breaks of the Missouri and clean out the core of rustlers. Jeff here is familiar with the area, and knows the

whereabouts of the main troublemakers. We hope to bring them back alive, if possible, dead if need be. Either way, they'll become an example that might make the more fainthearted among them think again before rustling any more stock."

Hunt rolled a cigarette as he talked; now he twisted it, set it on his lip, and fired it with a sulphur match. He looked squarely at McCan.

"We want you to be part of that group, Luke. It's specially selected, handpicked, secret. You're a man we can trust, and you can take care of yourself. Plus, you know the region firsthand—at least a little—and you know the kind of people we'll be facing. It could be dangerous, but I'm asking you just the same: will you ride with us?"

Before McCan could answer, Avery said, "And can you keep your mouth shut about it?"

The words riled McCan, but before he could answer, Hunt spoke again. "Jeff talks a little too straight sometimes, Luke, but he's got a point. This gets out, it would ruin it. Maybe cost some lives. Now, what's your answer?"

He tried not to show it, but McCan was flattered he had been asked. He accepted solemnly, and the others looked pleased, except for Avery, who seemed indifferent. Tackett and Hunt shook McCan's hand, but Avery didn't extend his. He was a droopy-eyed, sneering fellow McCan found inherently repulsive.

Hunt turned to more mundane talk. He quizzed McCan about his work, the condition of the cattle, the adequacy of the grass and water. McCan gave a report; then asked about news from Timber Creek. He was thinking of Maggie, but did not mention her.

"We got us a new town getting started right there," Tackett said.

McCan expressed amazement, but Tackett nodded

and went on, "A man name of Rodney Upchurch has come up from Milestown, and once the winter breaks, he's putting up a big store. Upchurch's Emporium, he'll call it, just like the one in Milestown. Figures he can make a pile off the ranchers and get some other folks to start up businesses, move some houses in, start up a new community. The word is he'd like to have it named after himself. One thing I'll say, he's a real character, sort of a city type, all bouncy and starry-eyed. He'll have to prove himself to me."

Hunt smiled. "Dan's a skeptic. But this fellow is onto something, I think. Run a few supplies in from Milestown by freight wagon, and people will be glad to take them off his hands."

"Where will it be?" McCan asked.

"Within view of Maggie's house," Hunt said.

"How is Maggie?"

"Fine. Doing fine." Hunt smiled quickly, a forced effort. He averted his eyes and put on his hat. "We got to be going."

"Wait a minute," McCan said. "Is something wrong with Maggie?"

Hunt and Tackett exchanged glances. Hunt said, "No. She's fine, like I said. And we really do need to go. If we don't get back out to you before spring, just come on in when it looks like the snow is done."

They went out the door and mounted. McCan, knowing he had not been told all, went to Hunt and asked again about Maggie. Hunt paused, looked him in the eye, and said, "Rodney Upchurch is courting her. Has been since he came. And that's about all there is to it."

McCan looked at him silently, then nodded. He felt something like a pig of hot iron doing a slow roll in his stomach.

The three rode off, Hunt and Tackett together, Avery slightly behind, spine bent and shoulders slumped as blue cigarette smoke trailed after him, puffed out steady as the belches of a train stack.

For the rest of the winter McCan did not see another human being. He was glad of it.

Upchurch had wasted no time. As McCan rode home, the last real snow a memory of two weeks back, the framework of a large building stood starkly against the sky. It stood on a rise about a half-mile from Maggie's cabin, and swarmed with workmen.

McCan admired one thing about Upchurch, even though he had not met him—a venture like this took grit. The store was miles from the nearest town, lonely and isolated in the middle of cattle range. Yet the notion was sensible. Many who lived here made it to Milestown maybe once or twice a year. A closer outpost would be a luxury. Upchurch might just succeed.

Too bad.

Something drew McCan's gaze northward. Standing there, in brand-new riding clothes, was Maggie. McCan's fingers tightened on the reins; he suddenly was aware of his unshaven face and dirty, smelly clothes.

But he rode to her. She saw him, and her eyes grew wide, but it did not seem a look of pleasure.

McCan dismounted and walked to her. "Hello, Maggie."

"Luke. How have you been?"

He wanted very badly to take her in his arms, but he couldn't. "Cold, mostly. Mighty cold."

"Did you read the books I gave you?"

"About two times each. It made a lot of difference."

Here I am, talking to Maggie, and it's like I'm chatting with a stranger in a tea parlor.

She smiled at him. A distant smile, almost formal.

"There's a store being built here," she said.

"I heard. Why are you out here, Maggie?"

Her smile became tighter, more artificial. "Waiting for someone."

A buggy clattered up behind McCan. He turned and saw a slender young man in a derby and a tailored brown suit expertly brake the rig. The man jumped lithely from his seat and trotted toward McCan, hand already extended. He was all teeth and sparkling eyes and the scent of bay rum.

"Rodney Upchurch, sir," the newcomer said. He pumped McCan's hand firmly. "Have you come looking for work?"

A burst of fury struck McCan. His fist clenched, began to go back. But Maggie's presence stopped him.

Upchurch finally dropped his hand, but kept the smile. He turned to Maggie and took her hand. *Moves like a nervous rooster*, McCan thought.

"Hello, dear," Upchurch said. He bent stiffly from the waist and kissed her cheek. She dropped her eyes.

"Thank you for waiting, dear," Upchurch said. "We'd best be getting on before it's any later." He tugged at her hand and pulled her toward the buggy. He flashed his smile at McCan again. "I'm sorry you didn't come earlier, when there was still work to be had," he said. "If you'll tell me your name, I'll be glad to keep you in mind."

What came into McCan's mind could not be vented in front of Maggie Carrington. He turned away and went to his horse. He rode toward Timber Creek, and did not look back as he heard the buggy rattle away in the opposite direction.

CHAPTER 16

For the next three weeks, McCan stayed to himself.
He volunteered for jobs that took him away from the
ranch, away from other people, and when he was not
gone, he remained aloof. At times he reminded himself
of Ben Weaver, back on the Deadwood freight run.

He saw Maggie only at deliberately great distances.
The thought of her stabbed him every morning and
stole his rest at night. He began gambling again, slipping off to poker games in back rooms or organizing
his own in the bunkhouse. But his work did not suffer.
Pain only concentrated his efforts at whatever he did,
and he worked with great intensity.

Meanwhile, the courtship of Maggie and Upchurch
progressed. So also did the work on the Emporium.
Behind it, Upchurch built a house; not a log or rough-
lumber hut, but a real, solid home built of high-grade
finished lumber, and with a metal roof.

Upchurch moved into the house when it was nearly
completed. He lived in a single room at first, with a
large window that faced west, and he developed a

habit of watching the sunset through that window. About a week after he moved in, he noted a rider on the hill, looking down at him. The next night he was there again, then the next, and the next. And one night he was gone.

Upchurch heard a pounding at his door. *Maggie*. He went to the door and flung it open.

Luke McCan—drunk—walked in, pulled back his fist, and left Upchurch on the floor, mouth bloodied.

"Next time, I'll carve you like a dead beef," he said.

Upchurch didn't get up until he was gone.

McCan returned the next day and apologized. Upchurch just looked at him, then had him arrested.

McCan lay in a cell in Milestown and watched a spider busily wrapping a fly in his web in the corner. A cigarette burned unheeded on his lip until the heat made him spit it out. He then saw Abe Hunt at the cell door, looking grimly at him.

"I'd invite you in, Abe, but the door seems to be jammed shut," McCan said.

"I've got a key," Hunt said. He turned the lock and entered. "If you want to trounce me and take it, go ahead. I hear you're good at trouncing men unexpected."

"If you've come to fire me, do it and spare the sermon," McCan said.

"I ain't come to fire you, though I should. I've come to get you out."

"Out? How?"

"Upchurch has decided not to hold it against you. He's not taking it to court."

"Why?"

"It seems somebody talked to him, made him decide to go easy on you."

Maggie. The thought just made it worse.

"Let's go, then," McCan said. He took his hat and pushed past Hunt and out the cell door.

Hunt had brought McCan's horse. As they rode, Hunt said, "Remember what we talked about in the line camp?"

McCan nodded.

"In a few days, there will be a few men riding in, one and two at a time, to that old line camp at the bluffs. You know the place. They'll come that way to avoid attention, and they'll come quietly. You'll be one of them."

"Who else?"

"You'll know them when you see them. I'll be there."

"And then?"

"And then I wish I knew. Maybe an easy time. Maybe something a lot rougher."

They reached a hill nearby Upchurch's Emporium. They had ridden all day, and were tired. McCan halted his mount. Sunset gilded the land, the nearly completed store building, and Upchurch's house behind it. Down a new road, a line of freight wagons rolled in. The creaking of their wheels sounded mouse-like across the distance.

"Looks like Upchurch's stock is arriving," Hunt said.

"Yeah." The sight brought memories to McCan: the roll into Deadwood; the death of Bob Webster, then Walter Black; the departure of Caleb Black for a vengeance hunt that had only brought him greater loss.

A door opened and closed below. In the dying daylight Upchurch emerged, a lantern in his hand, Maggie beside him. Upchurch waved the lantern at the incoming freighters, a glowing pendulum of light etching a line through the dusk.

"That little lady down there—she's your problem, huh?"

It was a more perceptive judgment than McCan would have expected from Abe Hunt. "I think it's me that's the problem," he said. "Let's go home."

They spurred their mounts toward Timber Creek.

Maggie Carrington awoke the next morning to the sound of someone approaching outside. She dressed quickly, combed her hair, and went to the door.

It was Luke McCan. She threw a shawl about her shoulders and pulled it tight, then stepped outside and waited for him.

"Maggie," he said. He touched his hat.

"Luke." There was ice in her voice.

"You heard about what I did to Upchurch?"

Her silence was colder than her voice had been.

"It was a fool thing. I'm sorry about it. I tried to tell him that, but he wouldn't listen. I'll go and try again."

"Don't," she said. "For God's sake, just leave him alone."

"Whatever you want."

She pulled the shawl tighter, seeming to shrink within it. Her face was very white.

Luke said, "There are things I wanted to be different. Maybe I was the only one who did. But it makes no difference. I'll be leaving here soon."

"Where will you go?"

"Does that matter?"

She seemed again to withdraw from him. It made him feel like a leper.

"No, I suppose it doesn't," she said.

McCan studied her white face, trying to remember how she had looked to him before, but he couldn't. "Good-bye," he said, and rode away.

She called after him, "I'm going to marry him, Luke."

McCan would not look back. He rode until she was far behind, out of view; then he stopped. He looked eastward, considering very seriously just riding until he was lost somewhere in Dakota. Riding off and never coming back. But no—he had promised to do a job for Abe Hunt.

Do it he would. When it was done, he would be free. He thought about that for a time, waiting for it to make him feel better, until finally he was weary of waiting.

PART III

MISSOURI BREAKS MASSACRE

CHAPTER 17

McCan rode alone, wondering what was coming and why he had agreed to take part. Really, he knew why: because Abe Hunt had asked him. And because he really had nothing else better to do with his life at the moment.

Funny thing, he mused. Not that many years ago he had been a green tinhorn fumbling with a new Colt pistol in Deadwood, clumsy and unable to protect himself and his friend from a cheap bumbler who was hardly a better marksman than he. He never would have thought, in those days, that he would ever ride into a vigilante effort, one that could be quite dangerous.

Vigilantism was on the rise at the moment. A lot of whispers, a lot of talk that drew public frowns from the cattle barons, but private smiles—McCan hadn't been so preoccupied as to miss that. Of late, bodies had been found swinging from cottonwoods by the Missouri, and bands of riders had been seen in the night.

McCan rode to the rim of a valley. It stretched out like a wide basin, rising into reddish bluffs on the far side, dotted throughout with scraggly brush. Below was the old line camp that was his goal. It was a particularly crude one and seldom used, built of the roughest logs, some with branches intact and groping wildly from its walls. There was a log corral nearby; three horses were in it.

McCan began his descent, wondering who waited below. He felt eyes on him.

When he was within three hundred feet of the camp, a husky black man appeared in the doorway. It was Bill Webster. McCan felt a burst of relief. If Bill, clear-headed as he was, had agreed to become involved in this, maybe everything was square. Then he realized that Bill might be just as lacking in information as he was.

"Have a hard ride?" Bill Webster asked.

"No problems."

McCan peered into the cabin and saw the shadowed form of Jeff Avery. *Lizard in a hole*, McCan thought. There were others with him, but McCan could not recognize them.

He dismounted and led his horse to the corral. He gave it water, removed the saddle and bridle. He hung the latter on one of the branches jutting from the cabin, and the former over the fence with the others.

The cabin smelled earthen, and was cool. A pungent scent of strong tobacco hung inside. Avery's cigarette butts lay by the dozens amid amber splatters of spittle on the floor. Avery reclined on a bunk that hung on rusted chains angled over to the log wall. He eyed McCan, who greeted him. Avery blinked back.

"Luke, this is Jed Strout, boss of the Lazy Arrow. And Solomon Smith and J. W. Anderson, same spread," Bill said. "This is Luke McCan, a good friend."

Hands went out, were shaken. There was tension here, palpable nervousness that exhibited itself in fingers a bit too stiff, grips too tight, nods of greeting too quick. Only Avery seemed calm and detached, his eyes in their usual droop, his lip in its usual snarl, defying anyone to move or impress him.

McCan sat in a corner and rolled a smoke. By now the sun was bloody in the sky, the cool night descending.

Abe Hunt arrived the next day, and with him was Tackett. McCan was glad to see them; their mere presence gave comfort and a promise of restraint in the conduct of the mission.

Hunt addressed them all. "Thank you for coming. You did it quiet, like we asked, and that's good. This is a serious business, maybe a dangerous one. But we're no lynch mob—not unless we're forced to be. We've been doing a lot these past months to trace down the points from where the worst of the rustlers operate, and we plan to move into those points quietly and quickly, taking prisoners. If they resist, we shoot them down. If they don't, we take them alive. That's the rule we'll abide by.

"Jeff Avery has done the background work, locating points for our raids and such as that. Listen to him, and he'll guide you well.

"There could be trouble, but you're men who can handle that. Otherwise you wouldn't have been chosen. But if anybody doesn't want to come along, now is the time to leave. It won't be held against you."

He paused. No one moved. The leather-faced ranch boss smiled. "Good."

Avery began talking, laying out details, background, plans. He was a vulgar man, obscene in speech and manner, and talked in ways that hinted at something other than the peaceful venture Hunt envisioned. Nothing overt—just hints, words and phrases that drew sharp glances from Hunt. Avery softened his words in response, until finally Hunt seemed satisfied again.

But Bill Webster leaned over and whispered to McCan, "There's a man with a personal grudge."

At noon they rode out, taking it slow, moving in a line toward the Missouri. Avery led them, cutting through gullies and behind hills so their course was hidden. But the farther they rode, the more unsettled McCan felt.

Don't turn coward, he told himself. But it wasn't cowardice. More like intuition, forewarning.

That night they bedded down in a grove, the men taking turns at watch. McCan awoke when Bill Webster bolted up, pushing back his blanket.

"What is it, Bill?"

"Oh, Lord," Bill said. "It was just a dream. Thank God."

"What was it?"

"That we was dead. All of us, bloody and dead."

McCan lay back down. "Oh."

CHAPTER 18

There had been a cabin here once, but it was now, for the most part, a relic. The roof had collapsed and its wood had been used for fires, and two runs of upper logs had been cannibalized in the same manner. Now only canvas covered the top, but the cabin obviously was occupied, just as Avery had said.

"Good spot for rustlers," he said to Hunt as they watched the gaping door of the building. "Hidden away, and nobody even knows it's being lived in."

"Which are these?" Hunt asked.

"Leroy Bain and his boys. Small-time stuff before, but now they're tied in with bigger operators. They've led upwards of twenty rustled herds across the border into Canada."

Across the clearing from the cabin was a small stable and a corral. The remnants of a haystack were scattered up against the cabin wall.

At Avery's direction, the men divided into two groups and crept down separately, drawing closer to the cabin. McCan, Hunt, Bill, and Tackett comprised one group; Avery and the rest the other. They moved quickly but quietly, then crouched and watched the cabin from both sides.

A man came out. He wore filthy long underwear with a missing backflap. His hair was matted from sleep. He was rolling a cigarette in one hand and using the other to open the fly of his underwear and relieve himself just outside the door.

"Now there's a trick for you," Tackett whispered.

Avery shouted, "Leroy!"

Cigarette makings and spray went everywhere. Hunt smiled; Avery had obviously timed his yell for just that effect. But the man in the long underwear didn't remain flustered for long; he vanished into the dark cabin, and a moment later a rifle muzzle slid out the front window.

"Who are you?" he shouted.

"Get out of the cabin—there's thirty of us out here!" Avery yelled back. "Six of us are deputy marshals, ten are soldiers, and the rest kill for fun."

"I recognize your voice, Jephthah Avery!" Leroy Bain shouted. McCan glanced at Hunt; the ranch boss's eyes narrowed at the realization of Avery's familiarity with Bain. "I never figured you'd have the guts to come 'round here no more!" Bain continued.

"Why does he know him?" McCan asked, but Hunt waved off the question.

"Bring out your boys and drop your guns, or we'll roast you alive in there," Avery said.

Bain fired, the shot ripping the cottonwoods and sending the raiders ducking. But it was a symbolic shot; Bain obviously could not see his targets.

Suddenly another shot jolted out, this one fired by Jeff Avery. The slug shattered part of the frame of the window from which Bain had fired.

Hunt swore and said. "Why'd he do that?" Then

he shouted, "Give it up, Bain, and there'll be no more shooting." Hunt glared across the distance at Avery.

Suddenly the canvas roof was in motion; it bulged upward, then down again. Somebody had slipped over the back wall, hidden between the top run of logs and the edge of the canvas sheet. McCan saw a man dart into the rocks and brush behind the cabin.

"One's gone!" Strout shouted.

Leroy Bain fired again, this time with better aim. Dirt kicked up near Strout, who was crouched near Avery. Reacting, Strout lost his balance and fell back on his rump. Bain fired again, and Strout grabbed his shoulder.

"Oh, no," Hunt said. He raised his rifle and fired at Bain.

McCan and the others did the same, and McCan knew what Hunt was thinking even as they did so: the peaceable intent of the venture was now moot. With the first spray of lead, a tone had been set. Now there was only one thing to do: fight the best fight they could.

They fired again and again toward the cabin, joining slugs in a volley that threw out chinking and rattled against rotting logs. The canvas bulged again—another one going over the back wall—but this time Avery fired. The bulge jerked and disappeared as the climber fell back inside the cabin.

Bain's voice called out: "You've hit my boy! We're giving up! Coming out!"

Bain's rifle flew out of the window a moment later.

"Thank God," Hunt breathed.

Bain came to the door, hands upraised. "You shot my boy," he said again. "He's bleeding bad."

Jephthah Avery raised his rifle and fired. Leroy Bain fell dead with a bullet through his heart.

Avery stood and rushed across the clearing. As the

others watched, stunned, Avery stepped over Bain's body and entered the cabin. There was a muffled yell, then another shot.

Avery emerged from the cabin with a grin on his face and his rifle raised triumphantly in the air.

Jed Strout, whose wound was superficial, sat in the corner of the cabin and stared at the blood where the youngest Bain had died. Strout was a quiet man, gentle by nature, and it was obvious to McCan he was trying hard not to cry. McCan didn't blame him.

"Do you know what you've done?" Hunt boomed at Avery. "You know that you've violated everything we set out to do? Turned this into a mission of murder?"

"It wasn't just *me* shooting at Leroy," Avery said. "Besides, he shot at us first."

"He was *surrendering*, Jeff! Nobody but you shot at him then. He had no gun. And it was worse, what you did to the boy—shooting a dying young fellow you had no call to kill."

"It was mercy," Avery said, "He was suffering and I spared him."

"Seems to me this Leroy Bain knew you right well," Tackett cut in. "You wouldn't have killed him to shut him up, would you?"

Avery's expression darkened. "I don't like your tone, fat man. If you're accusing me of—"

"Of murder. You're worse than the rustlers you're hired to take care of."

"I'll kill you for that," Avery said.

"When? When I'm unarmed somewhere, or lying on a floor bleeding to death? That's the way you kill, ain't it, Avery? You take me on man-to-man, and I'll feed you your own privates."

Avery lunged at Tackett, who seemed to expand to

bear-size, arms stretching out toward his attacker. But Hunt put himself between the men, pushing Avery back to his seat. McCan jumped in to restrain Tackett. Strout bowed his head and lost the battle against tears.

Bill Webster came through the door. "They're buried. What now?"

"I don't know," Hunt said.

"I never wanted to be part of no killing party, Mr. Hunt," Bill said.

"None of us did. Or maybe *one* did—Avery, was this your plan from the start? Kill off those you had a personal grudge against?"

"I'm a range detective, and a good one," Avery said. "I don't know why you're worked up. I know you've lynched rustlers yourself, Abe!"

"When we knew a man was guilty, and when there was no other way to do justice," Hunt said.

Bill Webster said, "Maybe we ought to turn back and just keep quiet."

"You're forgetting one thing," McCan said. "The first Bain boy got away. And he heard his father call Avery's name."

Avery went white. "We got to track him down and kill him."

"Want to murder another one?" Tackett said.

"You don't understand," Avery said, talking scared. "Bain had friends, men who follow the law of the feud. They'll come after me."

Rain began pelting the canvas above. It grew dark outside, and soon water fell in sweeping sheets across the prairie. It blew through the door on the back of a cold wind.

"We're stuck here awhile," Hunt said. "This could last the rest of the day."

The conversation waned. Hunt brooded, his lip curled. The others huddled in corners and along the walls. Avery paced about, fidgety and stripped of his normal cocky sneer.

The rain did not stop until night. Thick clouds blew gouts of water all day and brought the darkness early. Avery stopped pacing and sank into a sullen heap among the others. Hunt chewed slowly on a piece of jerked beef.

"There's only one thing to do," Hunt said at last. "Just what Bill said—go home and keep quiet. It's our best bet."

"I can't do that, Abe," Avery said. "Them that Bain was friends with, they'll come after me."

"That's your problem, then," Hunt said.

Avery's face went grim. "I'll name every mother's son of you to them," he said.

Tackett stood, a looming form in the little cabin. "I can snap his neck right here, Abe," he said. "Just give the word."

"Sit down, Dan," Hunt said. "Just sit down and let a man think."

They passed the night on the cabin floor, not sleeping. Morning broke, moist and golden, and Bill Webster was first to rise. He stepped out the door and stretched, and then he froze.

He went back inside. "Luke, Abe—look at this."

They went to the door. On the hillside, backed by the rising sun, was a long line of riders. Stock-still, side by side, and they were armed.

CHAPTER 19

From the shadows of the cabin the group watched the silent, unmoving riders. There were fifteen of them, most with rifles resting butt-down against their thighs, and all their intended victims knew why they brandished the weapons: to let fear get a firmer choke hold, for frightened men died with greater suffering.

"The Bain boy's out there," Avery said. "I never would have figured him to get such a group so quick."

Tackett said flatly, "When this is over, if both of us are alive, Avery, I'm going to kill you."

"He won't be alive to kill," Hunt said. "He'll be the first one they go after."

Avery made a tight, gulping noise in his throat. Tackett said, "Send him out, then. Feed him to them, and maybe that will satisfy them."

Hunt shook his head. "Not as long as I'm leading this affair. I don't do such as that to no man."

Jed Strout stood, took a deep breath. "Well, I'm not going to sit and wait for them. I'm riding out of here."

"They'll nail you dead first thing," Hunt said.

"They might. But if I stay, I'll be no better off. Maybe all they want is Avery. They might let me through."

Hunt slowly nodded. "They might at that."

"I don't think so," McCan said. "They'll be after all of us. Every one of us fired on this cabin, and the one that got away probably doesn't even know who killed his father and his brother."

"You can argue if you want," Strout said, "but I'm riding out. Sol, are you with me?"

Solomon Smith said, "If you ride, I ride."

"Anyone else?"

Nobody moved, and Strout nodded. "Sol, it's you and me." Decision seemed to have brought him courage—no tears now.

Strout and Smith walked to the door and held their rifles high, then laid them down in the doorway. Together they walked toward the little stable. In a few minutes they were riding slowly toward the line of horsemen.

The riders did not react in any visible way across the distance. Smith and Strout drew nearer, riding stiffly. McCan thought his heart would burst from his chest, and tension took his breath.

"They've reached the line," Hunt said.

Strout and Smith stopped, and for a time no one on the slope moved. It was evident they were talking, but nothing could be heard. Then, amazingly, the line of riders parted, and Smith and Strout passed through. The horsemen shifted position and watched them ride away—and when Bill Webster saw none of them looking at the cabin, he said, "I'm going over the wall to get the horses saddled. We can get out, maybe. Ride away."

He grabbed a chair, placed it against the wall, and slid up and out, just as the first Bain boy had done earlier. Behind the cabin, he slipped into the brush and crept to the stable.

McCan saw one of the riders signal. He thought for a moment that Bill had been spotted. But the signal had a different meaning. Two riders raised rifles and fired in the direction Smith and Strout had gone. Two shots, and that was all.

"God rest them, and thanks be they had no wives," Hunt said.

On the hill, the rider signaled again and the group divided. They moved in opposite directions along a line parallel to the cabin front, then each line cut toward the cabin through the protecting cottonwoods.

"It's starting," Hunt said. "Dividing for the kill."

As he spoke, a shot roared and a slug smacked the wall behind him. Every man in the cabin dropped and began searching for fighting position.

It was hard to find in the cramped quarters, for only the doorway and window afforded outlets. Gunfire pelted the cabin. Bullets whizzed through the doorway, the window, dug up the dirt floor, kicked out wood chips from the rear wall.

One slug tore out a line of chinking on the front wall, leaving a space about three feet from the floor—wide enough to accommodate a rifle barrel. McCan thrust out his Winchester and fired. One of the riders gripped his stomach and fell; his horse ran wildly back up the slope.

Several of the attackers dismounted, tied their horses in the most protected spots available, and worked down through brush and cottonwoods, still divided into two uneven lines. They peppered fire onto the cabin, making the canvas roof dance. With every tear, more light streamed in, its shafts dimmed by the gunsmoke and dust polluting the cabin's hot atmosphere.

McCan thought of Bill and darted to the southern wall. He pushed out chinking with his rifle butt and looked toward the stable.

Bill was in there, a vague shadow moving among the frightened horses. McCan saw him slide a saddle onto one of the mounts. Little gunfire struck the stable; the attackers apparently did not know it had a human occupant, and likely were hoping to preserve the horses for booty or trade.

But now a man slipped toward the stable through the grove. McCan strained his eyes, burning from gunsmoke and dust, and recognized Todd Feeney. He thrust his rifle barrel through the crack, took careful aim, and Feeney fell, with his side pierced. He kicked twice, fired a shot into the air, and lay still.

Meanwhile, Bill had saddled another horse. If the defenders could buy him enough time, perhaps he could ready enough mounts to give them a chance for escape—*if* they could vault the back wall or race across from the front without being shot down and safely make it to the stable.

Hunt and Tackett were busy at the front window. They took turns rising and firing, ducking down alternately to give the other his chance. They were an effective team—three bodies sprawled outside so attested. Tackett breathed heavily, choking in the grit and smoke. But Hunt was utterly calm, moving up and down like a machine, aiming, firing, levering his rifle as he came down again.

Avery was at the front door, left side, J. W. Anderson at the right. They worked independently and connected on fewer shots than did Hunt and Tackett. Still, Avery had killed one man, and Anderson had wounded another.

The original attacking force of fifteen had been reduced to nine, one of them wounded. Still, those in the cabin were outgunned, and Bill was too busy in the stable to fight. McCan saw another man creeping toward the stable and he fired; dirt spat up at the man's feet, and he jumped behind a mound of rock for cover.

Avery yelled, "I got Bain!" McCan turned. Avery crouched beside the door, grinning broadly; then suddenly the top of his head was gone, and his body pitched across the room. The grin remained, now ghastly in death.

"Never a better deserved slug through the brain," Tackett said.

"But one less man for us," Hunt responded.

Anderson shouted, "They've got fire!"

A flare arced across the background of the cottonwood tops, and something thumped onto the canvas above. A smoldering spot appeared where the torch lay, a little seep of smoke came through the underside, and then the canvas began to catch.

McCan grabbed the chair from which Bill had vaulted the back wall and moved it to the center of the room. He climbed onto it, but suddenly his leg went numb and he fell. Blood ran down his trousers— a slug had cut a clean notch just above his knee. Wincing, he forced himself up again and grabbed at the torch through the smoldering hole left by the flame.

He hoped enough moisture remained from last night's rain to keep the fire from spreading, but the sun had dried the old and brittle canvas. What was worse, the torch was drenched in coal oil that spilled, flaming, across the cloth. McCan got the torch and tossed it to the floor, but the canvas was in flames. Then came two more arcs of fire, two more thumps on the cloth above. Finally, a whiskey bottle filled with coal oil, a flaming wick in the neck, landed on the canvas. A slug shattered it, and fire was everywhere.

McCan leaped down just as a bullet cut one of the chair legs in half. He spilled awkwardly to the side and then across Anderson. He rolled off and bounded up, and Anderson recovered as quickly. Anderson drew a careful bead on a figure outside, fired, and dropped him; then a bullet pierced his neck and he fell back on the fallen torch, his hands at his throat and his back smothering out the flame. He did not move again.

By now the cabin was filled with a thick, black, choking smoke—and the canvas above raged with fire.

"Over the back!" Tackett shouted. He leaped toward the back wall and hung his hands on the top run, but the flaming canvas dropped on him and he fell back, two bullets piercing him before he struck the ground.

CHAPTER 20

"Dan!" McCan shouted.

He pushed aside the big piece of flaming canvas with his rifle and uncovered Tackett. The big man still breathed, but his eyes were glazed, and blood gushed from the two holes in him.

Behind McCan, Abe Hunt screamed. It was a grossly unnatural sound. McCan turned and saw Hunt beating at flames that crept up his trousers, then ignited his shirt. McCan ran to him and also beat at the fire, but it was too late. Hunt lost his head and ran out the door, where multiple shots felled him. He dropped to his knees; a final shot ended his suffering.

"Luke!" McCan heard Bill's voice from the southern side of the clearing. A sudden burst of gunshots came from the corral, a fusillade that seemed unending.

McCan returned to Tackett, and with strength he did not realize he had, hefted the bulky, limp body to the top of the back wall. The canvas was gone now, so Tackett's body rested a moment in full view of the attackers. McCan, too, was exposed. Bullets pounded the logs around him as he pushed Tackett across and behind the wall.

A slug tore at McCan's arm, creasing the skin. McCan fired at a man who had reached the doorway and aimed at him with a pistol. The man took the shot in the chest, dropped the pistol, and fell.

McCan yelled as he vaulted and grabbed the top of the wall. He clambered clumsily upward, losing his rifle in the process, and reached the top. From there he leaped over and landed beyond Tackett.

Bill Webster, who had just fought his way across the corral with two horses strung behind him, came to him and said, "Mount up!"

McCan did, moving in a surreal daze. He leaned across the saddle horn, then coaxed his horse across the corral, with no idea where to go from there. His horse overran another gunman who met him at the corner; the hooves pounded his body into the dirt. McCan galloped the horse across the open space and jumped the fence.

He faced three men there, all aiming weapons at him. He crouched low and went for his own pistol. They fired, he fired, and suddenly he was through, un-hit. Whether he had wounded or killed any of the three he did not know, and he did not turn to see. He spurred his mount into a run.

He had no sense of time or distance. His horse ran on; wind rushed by his face. He kept low in the saddle, hurting now, blood dripping down his leg.

He felt the wind of a slug at his ear. He looked across his shoulder and saw three riders coming fast after him. One was far closer than the other two.

McCan triggered off an unaimed shot over his shoulder. The report deafened him, and smoke prickled his face.

He could not see Bill or Tackett. He fired another shot, and the man behind him yelled and fell from his horse. The others fired as a unit toward McCan; one bullet clipped off part of his hair, the other sliced through his shoulder and made him scream.

Ahead was a jumble of bare rock. He guided his horse through it, scrambling up a narrow passage as more bullets spanged around him. His horse was getting winded, but he pushed it hard. At the top, as the riders reached the base of the rocky knoll, McCan's mount stepped into a crevice and went down, trumpeting in pain. McCan pitched across to land face-down behind a boulder.

He reached for his pistol—*gone!* He saw it in the dust near his fallen horse. He went for it, stumbling on his wounded leg.

Before he could reach it, one of the riders topped the rocks. McCan saw his grin as he leveled down, ready to fire. McCan dropped behind his horse; the slug went into it rather than him. The horse shuddered and died.

McCan could not reach his pistol, but he found a fist-sized rock. He stood and heaved it, hard as he could, as the gunman fed a new cartridge into his rifle chamber. The stone crushed the man's nose, and he fell back over the rump of his horse. McCan reached his pistol as the man pushed upward and went for his own. McCan put a bullet through the man's chest.

Then the second rider was up the slope. McCan aimed at him, squeezed the trigger, and heard an empty click. He tossed the pistol aside and went for the dropped rifle of the first rider. He almost had it when the second rider's horse reared and threw him. The man, though big, hit the ground on his feet, for he leaped when he saw he could not retain his seat.

Then he shouted and threw himself atop McCan. McCan went down, breath driven from him.

The man was heavy, and he drove sledgelike fists against McCan's kidneys. McCan's face ground against gravel and grit; his mouth filled with sand and blood. With a painful twist, he pushed the man off and himself up.

A boot caught him in the chest and he fell back. He saw then his attacker was Jack Parker.

He took the first blow but dodged the second, and Parker's fist cracked against rock. Parker yelled and grasped his damaged fingers. McCan said, "Jack, don't you know me?" and Parker started shouting curses. He reached for his side arm, and McCan rolled over a boulder and out of view.

Here the rocks leveled into a kind of small plateau, and farther on dipped up again into a stone ridge, jagged as a rusted knife. McCan ran for those rocks. A bullet thumped just behind his foot, and a second ricocheted off just ahead. Parker shot too fast and carelessly to connect; McCan made it to the rocks.

He was so tired he almost blacked out. He fell into a recess and panted; his lungs burned and his throat was raw. He found a stick, about four feet long and with good heft. It was a pitiful weapon against a six-gun, but he kept it, hoping maybe he could get behind or above Parker and clout his skull with it.

McCan rose to run, but the rocks were crumpled like wadded paper, and he had to clamber slowly among them. Another bullet smacked too close to him, and he hurried on over the boulders to a gradual upward slope of flat rock.

He ran, but saw a rider approaching from the right. Nowhere to go, no way to protect himself. He waited for the death shot, and then saw the rider was Bill

Webster. Riding double with him, amazingly, was a badly bleeding Dan Tackett.

McCan pointed toward the rock spine he had crossed. Parker climbed over it at the same time and triggered off another round. McCan's leg was shot from beneath him.

Bill drew his pistol and shot at Parker, but missed. However, Parker did turn and throw himself behind cover, buying McCan a few moments.

"Hide—I'll come back!" Bill yelled, and rode off with Tackett swaying behind.

McCan didn't blame him; Bill could do little else until Tackett was safely stashed somewhere. McCan tried to run on his wounded leg, but it was numb, and he did well to stand.

Parker came up and shot again, missed again, and when he pulled the trigger next, the gun was empty. He went after his pistol, but he had tied it down too tightly and had to fumble with the strap. McCan stumbled, rolled, half-walked, half-tumbled down the slope and threw his club into Parker's face. Parker still had not freed his pistol.

McCan used his good leg to lunge against Parker, and together they fell against abrading stone that took off skin. McCan clung to Parker, then pushed him back and started hitting.

He pounded Parker's face three times, and the big man pulled away, grabbing his nose. McCan kicked his belly by clumsily swinging his numb leg, and though he could not feel the impact, it must have been significant; Parker doubled over, and McCan brought his fists down on the back of his neck.

Parker did not get up. McCan took the dropped rifle and cracked the stock into Parker's skull. He looked around and saw Bill coming back, Tackett no longer mounted.

"Good to see you," McCan said as he hefted himself onto the horse's rump. When he was mounted, Bill guided the horse back the way he had come. From the corner of his eye, McCan saw Parker rise.

McCan shouted a warning into Bill's ear, but Bill did not understand. Parker freed his pistol from its holster—McCan cursed himself for not thinking to take it—and then McCan reached up and drew Bill's side arm.

He twisted in the saddle and fired at Parker as Parker fired at him.

Parker's shot missed McCan but struck Bill in the side. McCan's shot ripped through Parker's abdomen. Parker fell, and Bill slumped over the saddle horn. Too late, McCan saw they had reached the edge of a bluff about thirty feet high. Bill's shifted weight caused the horse to lose its footing, and it plunged with its two riders over the edge.

McCan blacked out, but came to moments later. He had not fallen to the bottom, but had lodged on a rock outcrop about halfway down. About half of him dangled over emptiness; the other half teetered in an uneasy balance on the rock. Below, he saw Bill's body sprawled beside that of the dead horse.

Something dripped onto him from above, splattering on his hand. Blood. McCan looked up. Jack Parker stood at the rim, pistol in hand, wavering like a drunk. He aimed and fired. McCan felt a hot poker ram through his shoulder as Parker died on his feet and toppled over on top of him.

McCan was dislodged and plunged with Parker's corpse to the rocks below. He landed on top of Parker, and that saved him.

Something moved nearby. He rolled over, the effort sending spasms of pain through him.

A man on a gray horse aimed a Spencer at him. It was Evan Bridger. McCan noted it dispassionately. The image of Bridger shimmered and danced away like a heat devil as McCan gave in to the darkness.

CHAPTER 21

Coming to was a slow rise through muddy water, a steady lightening, a murky disorientation and sense of disbalance. McCan stared upward at the underside of a brown peak of canvas, felt the breeze, and knew he was alive. He might have cried, but his eyes were crusted and tearless, and when he moved, the pain erased thoughts of all but itself.

A man's blurred face looked into his. "Hello, Luke."

McCan forced his eyes to focus. "Hello, Caleb."

McCan had whispered, but the effort tired him as if he had tried to shout. His body ached so badly he could hardly tell one limb from another.

"You're going to be fine, Luke. Just rest."

McCan slept and dreamed he was back in Deadwood. He woke up in darkness and asked for water. Black brought him a cup of it, and he sipped it slowly, washing the grit from his throat, the acid sourness from his tongue.

"I saw Evan Bridger," McCan said.

Black nodded, a suspicion confirmed. "I thought he was here. I'd have got to him if I'd moved a little faster."

Always the chase, McCan thought. *He'll chase Bridger right into hell.*

Rain whispered on the canvas. It cooled the air and soothed McCan. He lay with eyes shut and listened, not sleeping, not really awake. Caleb Black hunched over on the other side of the little tent, smoking a pipe and sometimes humming softly an old mountain melody.

Strength came slowly, but it came. Caleb Black took care of McCan with the devotion of a nurse, and a surprising gentleness for a powerful man whose once-smooth face now looked like a desert map, parched and windburned, lined from weathering and something that cut deeper even than that.

Luke McCan surmised as best he could what had happened after his pitch over the bluff, but mysteries remained.

"Did you find a black man at the bottom?" he asked Caleb.

"No. Only a big fellow, white, lying right under you."

"Jack Parker. There should have been a black man too. Bill Webster—Bob's brother. You remember Bob?"

"I do. The one the redheaded gunfighter killed."

"Jimmy Wyatt. And then Evan Bridger killed him."

Black merely nodded at the mention of his old foe. He bit the end from a cheap cigar and lit the smoke.

"Maybe Bill survived," McCan said. "What about a hefty fellow, even bigger than the one under me, probably shot two or three times. He would have been hid out somewhere close by."

"Nope. Just you and the dead one."

McCan was solemn. "So he's dead then. Probably died alone, wherever Bill left him."

That night they ate roasted rabbit and drank coffee. Black threw in a pinch of salt, just like he did back in Deadwood, and the taste, as familiar tastes and scents will, brought back vivid memories of those times. McCan realized he missed them, and said as much to Black.

"I know," Black said. "I think about those days myself. We've gone many a mile since then. Sometimes I wonder when it all will stop."

"When Bridger's dead. Or you."

"I reckon."

"Is it worth that much to you, Caleb?"

Black smiled. A pinched tightness at the edge of his lips made him look old: "No. Not really. But hate is a funny thing. It has a sweetness all its own. It's a deep spring to drink from, and when you do, you're thirsty for more."

McCan said, "I don't blame you, really. I'd do the same in your shoes. But this life is aging you fast. It'll kill you if keep on. I can see that."

"So you're a preacher now? When did you get the call?"

"Not preaching. Just common sense." McCan's wounds hurt again, and his voice grew tight. "Why didn't Bridger kill me, Caleb? I was in his sights when I passed out."

"Why does he do anything? He lives on impulses, whatever strikes at the moment. Why did he kill Jimmy Wyatt? Why did he murder a woman and an unborn baby who never did him no harm?" Suddenly Black's jaw trembled, his eyes brimmed. "If I could put a bullet through my brain and know it would kill him too, I'd do it. Without a thought."

There was silence. Black puffed his cigar furiously. McCan closed his eyes and tried to will away his hurting.

"Maybe when I'm all healed up and you've finished with Bridger, we can become partners again," McCan said.

"Doing what?"

"Anything. Running a store. Being ranchers. Sodbusters. Sheepherders. Selling bloomers to the females."

Black laughed. It was the first real laugh McCan had heard from him since the Deadwood days. It was good to hear, and made him laugh too, even though it hurt.

After a time, McCan quit numbering the days. He grew stronger as the pain went away. But he was in no hurry to return to Timber Creek, and one realization made him consider not returning at all.

Everyone back there certainly thought him dead by now. That gave a strange feeling of freedom. He could ride away, forget the ranch and Maggie and everything else, and start over again in some other place.

McCan thought of that, but he thought of it very little. Mostly he rested, ate, talked to Caleb, enjoyed the refuge and the quiet.

It was good to be here. Good to hide, good even to be dead in the eyes of the world.

That existence went on for several weeks, until one day, Caleb said it was time to go looking for Evan Bridger again.

CHAPTER 22

"You'll go back to Timber Creek?" Black asked.

McCan said, "I don't know. It depends on if you're willing to let me ride with you instead."

Black smiled thinly. "It's a hard road I travel, but suit yourself."

McCan's wounds were healed, but tender. He ached from the inside out, muscles stiff from lack of use. Black had found McCan a fine bay roaming near the battle site, but just saddling the horse winded McCan.

"Where will we go?" he asked.

"The Missouri Breaks. I know somebody who can put me on Bridger's trail, though he won't want to."

"What if he won't talk?"

"I'll persuade him."

They rode north to the river, then turned west along its course.

Four men played cards and drank whiskey in a low, wide cabin. Sunset flung magnificent purple-scarlet rays through the open westfacing door. Something blocked the light, and the men turned.

"Evening, gentlemen," Caleb Black said.

One of them stood and turned slightly to make sure Black saw the Texas Dragoon in his belt. "Who are you?"

"My name is Caleb Black." The man looked past Black to McCan, who was still mounted outside. Black said, "That's a friend of mine who's no concern to you."

"What do you want?"

"Not what—who. I'm looking for Cyrus Keye."

Another man stood. He was a six-footer, broad and muscled. His black beard swept halfway down his chest and ended in a gray flourish. "I'm Keye," he said.

"Well, Keye, you've got two options. The first is to give me some information."

"Or?"

"The second is to oblige me to drag your corpse to a ranch I know that pays good bounties for dead cattle thieves."

Keye filtered a smile through his drooping mustache. His black eyes flickered over the others; the other men stood.

"You're right entertaining, Mr. Black. But you got no call to talk so to good Christian folk."

"Which option, Keye?"

"You're wearing thin, Mr. Black," Keye said. "But I'm curious. What information do you want?"

"I'm looking for Evan Bridger."

Keye's brows lifted and lowered. "Why should I know where he is?"

"You're a knowing kind of man."

Keye nodded. "That I am. And I know you. You must be one hell of a crazy man to tail Evan Bridger all these years."

Black smiled. "That's right. I'm crazy enough to call

down four men at once too." He looked calmly from man to man. "It really ain't much of a challenge. Only two of you have half a chance, and that ain't enough. The other two have none at all."

Cyrus Keye laughed—big, booming guffaws. "Mr. Black, I kind of like you. You're as loco and reckless as I am. But I can't tell you nothing about Evan Bridger."

"Can't, or won't?"

"It's all the same."

"Then I'll have to kill you," Black said. Keye leaned back and laughed again. The man with the Dragoon drew; Black put a slug through his neck. Keye quit laughing, went for his pistol, and Black shot him to death. The other two toyed with the idea of drawing only a half-second, then forgot it.

Black waved his pistol at them. "Bridger?"

"He was here two days ago. He headed for Wolf Point."

"What else?"

"That's all I know."

Black thumbed the hammer; the men paled. "I swear it," one said. "We don't know nothing else."

"Then you're no use to me except bounty," Black said.

The first man spoke, "The only other thing was he looked like he was feeling poor. All washed-out and trembling."

"Where at Wolf Point was he going?"

"He runs with Crandal Booth. He's a woodhawk and a whiskey trader."

Black indicated the dead men. "Drag them out and put them over their horses."

The men obeyed, obviously very scared. McCan wondered what Black would do with them. He was stunned by the calm way he had dispatched the other two. Hard to believe this cold pistol fighter was the Minnesota wheat farmer who had dropped his tools on the boardwalk in Pierre.

When the men were finished, Black made them lie down and told Luke to guard them. Then Black found a rope and slung it over a jutting roof beam at the corner of the cabin. One of the men whimpered.

"Shut up—I ain't going to lynch you," Black said.

Two minutes later, the men dangled back-to-back from the beam, hanging by their wrists with their feet eight inches off the ground.

"You're going to leave us like this?" one said.

"Yep."

"It could be days before somebody comes along!"

"I suggest you try yelling—and hope whoever hears you ain't a cattleman."

Black and McCan rode toward the river, two dead bodies bouncing on the horses trailing them. When they were a few hundred yards from the cabin, the dangling men yelled. Their cries echoed off the bluffs across the river.

"What will happen to them?" McCan asked.

"They'll wiggle out after awhile. It'll probably cause me trouble later. I should've shot them, but I'm just too softhearted. And a soft heart ain't nothing but a headache."

CHAPTER 23

They took the dead men to a ranch house four miles eastward, and there a squint-eyed cattleman inspected the corpses and handed Black a wad of bills. Black pocketed the money and they rode away.

"That's the first bounty I've seen paid," McCan said.

"Bounty, lynching, shooting, burning, stock detectives—cattlemen use it all. But thieves don't stop. As long as there's cattle, there'll be rustlers."

They rode along the knobs and slopes bordering the Missouri. Cottonwoods grew thick over long stretches, gave way to barren dirt at others. As they progressed, the land inclined and the river banks steepened, pushing them farther inland. They saw no one except a distant raftsman, and heard nothing but the flowing of the water and the chop of a woodhawk's ax somewhere on the far bank.

In a thick grove of cottonwoods and poplars, they camped for the night, tired and dirty from the trail.

* * *

Something stirred on the border of McCan's dreams. Something rustled in the forest. He heard the whisper of stealthy footsteps and awoke. It was dark, the sky covered with clouds no starlight could penetrate. The fire was just a coal bed spitting up sparks when the breeze gusted.

McCan slid his hand to the rifle beside his bedroll. He listened, unmoving. Wind stirred the cottonwoods; branches creaked. Through slitted eyes, McCan scanned the forest as he pretended to sleep.

A shadow moved beyond the tree line.

McCan slid the cover back and rose. More movement—a vague shifting. He slid through the trees, levering the Winchester.

A figure whirled to face him. Eyes locked in the darkness.

"Lucky I didn't kill you," Black said.

"Don't flatter yourself."

Black lifted a finger to signal silence. Like McCan, he had a rifle. He crouched; McCan knelt beside him.

They peered into the empty campsite. A whirlwind, moist with river mist, swirled across the little clearing and sent embers spiraling. In that faintest of glows, they saw dark forms on the opposite side.

"Shoot?" McCan suggested in a whisper.

"Not yet."

The forms came closer, to the very rim of the clearing. Fireglow glinted on a shotgun barrel.

The shotgun blasted, lighting the camp like a lightning flash. McCan's bedroll took the charge, dancing up like a wraith.

Black raised his rifle and fired.

The shotgun roared again in return. McCan flattened on the damp earth; pellets scattered above him. He rose and darted to the right. Unseen branches slapped him.

McCan dropped behind a rock. Something moved several yards from him. He raised his rifle, but did not fire, for he realized Black was no longer with him. That might be him in his sights.

Gunfire slashed through the cottonwoods; McCan saw the disembodied flares. In them he picked out Black's shape, and two others near him. McCan aimed, but the forms shifted and he did not know friend from assailant.

Someone cursed; a rifle fired. The figures in the forest moved away from him. McCan pushed upward, over the rock, but his foot slid on the damp ground and he crashed down hard. His head struck something, night closed in, and he was out.

He came to moments, maybe an hour later. His head was bloody and throbbed. He struggled for perspective. He pushed up on his forearms and looked across the campsite, and suddenly his view was blocked by what appeared to be twin tree trunks. Focusing, he saw they were legs. His eyes lifted—a rifle butt descended toward his face.

He rolled to the side. The rifle butt struck rock; sparks jumped off the metal buttplate. McCan reached for his own rifle but did not find it. His attacker brought down his weapon again. Once more McCan rolled, then came to his feet. He ran, toward the river, and the man followed.

Weaponless, McCan felt like a declawed bear chased by hounds. Gravel tore like dull razors at his bare feet. He bit his lip and ran harder.

His toe stumped rock and he pitched forward, rolling onto his back as his attacker fired. The slug thunked into the ground beside his ear.

McCan leaped up as the man levered. He grabbed the rifle and pushed it aside, and with his right hand pounded first the man's stomach, then his mouth. The man grunted at each connection, then pulled the rifle free and swung it; the front sight ripped a cut across McCan's lip.

A pure anger, simultaneously primitive and righteous, filled McCan. He grasped the rifle and wrenched it away. Fighting with emotion rather than logic, he tossed it into the river, then drove his knee into the man's crotch.

He buckled; McCan joined his fists and brought them down on the back of the man's neck. Then McCan's old injuries flared, with new ones, in a burst of pain that took his consciousness. He fell beside the senseless form of his opponent.

He came to after several minutes, feeling sick. He pushed nearly upright. His assailant still lay unconscious near him.

McCan rolled him over; it was one of the men he and Black had left hanging back at the cabin. "Finally got mad enough to be brave," he said aloud. Then he rose and returned to the camp. Black was not there.

He went into the woodland and hid until morning, listening for Caleb, hearing nothing.

In the light of dawn he looked for his partner. Back at the river, the man he had fought was gone; McCan had not heard him rise and creep away.

McCan wanted to yell for Caleb, but could not risk it. So he walked silently until he found blood on the ground. It made a crooked trail to the river.

On the bank was a pink pool of bloodied water. Someone had knelt here to wash a wound. McCan examined the ground; there was a wide smudge in the thin mud. Maybe the mark left by a body that had collapsed into the water.

There was no body there now. The current must have carried it away.

Don't let it be you, Caleb. But McCan knew Black would have found him by now if he was able. He shook his head, and hot tears skimmed his eyes. He turned back to the camp in the cottonwood grove.

CHAPTER 24

McCan rode to Timber Creek in the night, but the moon was bright and lit his trail. The sleeping ranch was eerily beautiful beneath the vast sky. McCan had thought seriously of not returning here, but now that he saw it again, he was glad he had.

He rode to the corral and dismounted, then carried his saddle and gear to the stable. He walked to the bunkhouse, but did not enter. Instead, he sat by the door to wait for dawn. Entering now would bring only confusion, maybe fear, among those who thought him dead.

A few moments later, however, Stewart Biggs came to the bunkhouse door. He wore long underwear and looked like some gray ghost in the darkness. Biggs looked blankly at McCan, rubbed his eyes, and looked again.

"Thank God," Biggs said. "We had no hope for you."

"Sorry I roused you, Stewart. I planned to wait it out until morning."

"How did you make it through alive? Bill Webster said—"

"Bill? *Alive?*"

"Yes." Biggs spoke solemnly. "But things are bad for him. And for Dan Tackett, it's worse."

"Tackett is alive too?"

"Yes, but . . ." He stopped. McCan prompted him, but he said only, "Let me get my clothes. I'll take you to them."

McCan waited until Biggs reemerged, clothed and boots in hand. He sat on the ground and pulled them on. "I didn't wake up anybody. No point in stirring them just yet."

They rode east. "How *did* you survive, Luke?" Biggs asked.

"It's a long story I'll tell you sometime. Right now, I want to know about Bill and Dan."

"The short of it is, Dan lost his job—and more. You remember the little Iowan who hired you? He fired Dan. 'No vigilante works in my hire,' he says. Cuts him loose, and Dan in the shape he is."

"What do you mean?"

"We're here. See for yourself."

They came to a dark little hut, starkly outlined on the barren land. Biggs dismounted and knocked on the door. "Bill! It's Stewart. I've got somebody you'll want to see."

Bill Webster came to the door, eyes half-shut from sleep, expression confused. Biggs smiled and pointed to McCan. Bill looked at him a few moments silently. McCan dismounted, came to him, and thrust out his hand. Bill took it, his shoulders heaved, and he threw his burly arm around McCan.

"I didn't think you lived through it, Bill," McCan said.

"We hardly did. Tackett saved me. He dragged himself out from where I had put him, found me all battered up, and somehow put together a litter and rounded up a stray horse and got me home. And him half-dead himself. But he paid a price for it: his leg is gone. Got putrified, and they sawed it off soon as he got here."

Inside, they awakened Tackett, and McCan forced a smile despite the shock of the realization: Dan Tackett was dying. McCan knew it as soon as the lamplight played across the old cowboy's face. He was wan, losing weight, eyes sunken. There was an empty place beneath the covers where his left leg should have been.

"It's a miracle," Tackett said. "An answered prayer. I figured you for dead."

"I figured the same for you," McCan said.

"God was with us."

"I'm sorry about your leg, Dan."

"It don't matter. Soon I won't need this old body no more. He'll take me home with him."

He's turned religious, McCan thought. *Knows he's dying.*

"The ranch turned Dan away, I hear," McCan said to Bill when they had left Tackett. "How are you living?"

"I had to leave the Lazy Arrow to take care of Dan. We're living on pure charity. The Timber Creek boys slip out here and give a hand. John Weatherby brings us food. Even this house is on loan from Stewart—it was his brother's before he died. I'd look for work around here, but I'm all torn up inside, and Dan takes a lot of caring for. I got to be with him all the time."

McCan nodded. "I'll find a way to help. Count on it."

When McCan and Biggs returned to the ranch, McCan was greeted with awe and a few cheers. Disheartened though he was by the plight of Tackett and Bill Webster, McCan was overcome by the welcome.

He told how Caleb Black had saved him, and then apparently been killed at the river. Most of the men had heard of Black; his pursuit of Bridger had made him part of the folklore of the Territory.

When word reached the main house of McCan's return, he was sent for. He knew what to expect.

Henry Sandy awaited, a fop with spectacles on his narrow nose. He looked at McCan through the bottoms of the lenses, like a museum manager examining a butterfly on a pin.

"You are Luke McCan?"

"I am."

"You participated in the vigilantism to the north?"

"I did."

"You realize, then, that I must dismiss you at once."

"Well, I know you fired Dan Tackett. I don't expect better for myself."

"The Timber Creek Cattle Enterprise does not sponsor vigilante activity, and it does not take up arms against lawless men. That is the job of the law. This is a nation and a territory of laws."

"It's a territory of cattle thieves," McCan said. "And what do you mean, Timber Creek doesn't sponsor vigilantism? I took part at the request of Abe Hunt, *for* Timber Creek."

"Mr. Hunt went beyond his authority. Had he lived, I would have fired him first."

"Do your superiors back east know what you're doing?"

"I'm now the manager of this ranch. They don't need to know every move."

"Well, ranch manager, you can bet Abe Hunt wouldn't have done anything like what we did without the approval of the highest officers of the company. You'd best check to see whose side you're playing up to."

Sandy gave a sniffing little laugh. "You obviously don't comprehend the operation of this cattle company."

"Maybe not. But I understand cattlemen, and know you're not one. You're just a dried-up Iowa jackass who'll run this company broke before your bosses know you're doing it. Abe Hunt was the best cattleman on any spread within five hundred miles, and he did everything he could to keep that mission peaceful and law-abiding. It was a range detective carrying some old grudge who turned it into a war. You don't need to fire me. I wouldn't work for a gut-worm like you anyway."

Sandy's little black eyes glittered through his spectacles. "You're quite the speechmaker, Mr. McCan. But I think you need to leave now."

McCan suddenly thrust out his hand. Surprised, Sandy took it. McCan noted the softness of Sandy's hand, like a woman's.

"Apart from the fact you turn my stomach, there's no hard feelings on my part," McCan said. "But this is for Dan."

He drove his fist into Sandy's nose. The spectacles split at the nosepiece and lenses flew east and west. Henry Sandy flipped backwards over his desk and sprawled on the floor. McCan strode out of the room, whistling.

Mrs. Martha Hyatt
Independence, Missouri

Dear Martha,
    You've heard I am dead, so they tell me, so I suppose it would be appreciated by you to hear

I'm not. I don't know what all you were told about the circumstances of my supposed passing away, but I'll just tell you the basic facts—I came mighty close to dying, and some men with me did die. We were on a chase after some no-accounts and thieves, so I was on the right side of the law at least. I've done worse in the past as you well know.

I'm without any work right now and not sure just where I'll be going. I'm living with two friends, both good men who got hurt, just like me, and came close to not making it back, just like me again. There's one that will die yet, I think, and that's why I'm staying around for now. There is another tie holding me here too, but that is one of a different sort and her I don't want to discuss.

I will do well in some way or another and will let you know just as soon as I am settled differently. It may be I will come to see you soon but as of now I'm inclined to remain away until my times are better. Write me a letter so I can hear what your own circumstances are.

Your brother still living,
Luke

CHAPTER 25

—

Dan Tackett sang a hymn just before he died, clutching a Bible they left in his hand when they buried him.

McCan, never prone to cry, cried now. It was more than grief for Tackett alone. He mourned for Abe Hunt, for Caleb Black, for Maggie—all of them lost to him.

When it was over, McCan asked Bill, "Where will you go now?"

"Looking for work wherever I can find it."

"Need a partner?"

"Be proud to have one."

"Good. But there's something I need to do before we go."

They rode to Upchurch's Emporium. The store thrived; people, buggies, horses, wagons were everywhere. A blacksmith shop—new—operated nearby, plus a barber shop and tack store and horse trading pen. Three houses were under construction within view.

"Looks like there really *will* be a town here," McCan said.

They tethered their horses to the hitching post outside the Emporium. They walked inside and swept off their hats. An organic, marvelous smell filled the place—a mixed scent of leather, cloth bolts, candy, tobacco, spices, flour, gun oil.

Rodney Upchurch tended a customer in the back. McCan walked there and waited until Upchurch was finished. Bill wandered off in the meantime to inspect a shotgun he had admired a long time but never could buy.

Upchurch finished his business and saw McCan. His smile disappeared. McCan could not read his expression.

"Well," Upchurch said. "I see the stories *are* true. A man really can come back from the dead."

"I'd like to talk to you, Upchurch."

"Step into my office."

"No. Outside. If your buggy's handy, we'll take it."

Upchurch looked irritated but curious. He made a show of removing his apron, slapping it to the counter, and striding out the front door. McCan followed him. A few minutes later the two men were bouncing down the dirt road in Upchurch's leather-dashed buggy.

"What do you want from me?" Upchurch asked.

"First, I wanted to tell you again I'm sorry I attacked you. It was wrong."

"That's already forgotten. I didn't run you through court, did I?"

"I appreciate that too."

"This isn't what you came to talk about, McCan. You came to talk about Maggie."

"Yes."

Upchurch chuckled bitterly. "You know, I didn't even know you and Maggie had had a relationship until just a few weeks ago. When word came you were dead."

"How did you find out?"

"From Maggie. She . . . cried. I started asking questions."

"Cried." McCan shook his head and smiled sardonically. "Well, I'm capable of stirring something in her, at least." It was a private thought spoken out loud, and Upchurch didn't appear to appreciate it.

"Just what do you want from me?" he said.

"I'm not sure. Just to hear me out, maybe. I loved Maggie, you see. I *still* love her. But I'm not a fool. You've won her, which makes me the loser. But I want you to know this: if I could take her from you right now, I'd do it. And there's a part of me that will always resent you because that won't ever happen. It should have been me, not you." He paused. "I just needed to tell you that. Does that make any sense to you?"

Upchurch said, "Yes. More than you might think." He was silent awhile, then said, "I might be a fool for this, but—in two days, Maggie and I will be getting married. It will be an outdoor wedding, at the Emporium, and you're welcome to attend."

McCan nodded. Neither man spoke again until they were back at the store. McCan rejoined Bill. "We'll be staying on another day or two," he said. Bill started to ask a question, but noticed McCan's expression and held his peace.

It was more than a wedding. Typical of Upchurch's style, it was a three-fiddle party that drew people from fifty miles around. First came the ceremony, short but elegant by frontier standards. McCan stared at Maggie throughout, watching her being stolen from him while he stood helpless. When it was done, he turned away and went searching for spiked punch.

The party began. It was a fine setting: tables spread with white cloths and laden with washtubs of cold punch, heaps of roast beef, boiled potatoes, thick biscuits, hot ears of yellow corn, pies, cakes, gallons of steaming coffee, beer, jellies, big hunks of mold-pressed butter, puddings, sausages, and wild fowl.

The fiddlers sawed away. As darkness spread over the sky, out came paper lanterns. Dozens of couples danced—girls in their finest dresses, the ones they kept wrapped in muslin; men with new haircuts that raised their hairlines an inch above their ears and made them look like peeled onions. Their trousers were washed and pressed, their small-collared shirts with baggy sleeves starched and snow-white.

The scene was colorful, whirling, lit by the flaring lanterns. Children ran about. Boys wrestled on the fringes of the gathering, as others stood guard at the tables, charged with defense against dogs and flies.

McCan approached Bill Webster, his fourth glass of punch in hand. "Nothing at all to hold me here now," he said. "That was my last tie to Timber Creek."

"You're lucky and don't know it," Bill said. "Just like me. I came close to getting caught, but I didn't."

"What happened?"

"She decided she liked my brother Bob better than me, and she was after him like jaybird on a squirrel. That's why Bob run off to be a freighter. He never told you?"

McCan laughed and shook his head.

"It's the truth. After he was gone, she had no use for me. Took a cap-and-ball pistol and shot off half my little toe, and that's no lie."

"I'm glad you survived your love life, Bill."

The party went on. Upchurch and Maggie stood on

the store porch as a line of people greeted them. McCan had never seen her look as beautiful as she did now. Salt rubbed on a wounded heart.

McCan tossed down his final mouthful of punch. "Might as well give the couple our regards," he said.

Maggie smiled and took his hand when he came to her. "I'm so glad it wasn't true—about you being dead."

"I'm right pleased about that myself. Good luck to you, Maggie. I wish you happiness."

"I wish you the same," she said, and then she kissed him.

He wandered off alone to the south end of the store building, musing. The day was almost gone, only the faintest memory of daylight remaining. McCan heard a noise. Far down the road he saw a bobbing glow—a lantern held by a rider, it appeared. As it came closer he saw a wagon too. Both the rider and the wagon driver were rushing. McCan walked toward them and met them before they reached the party.

The rider with the lantern had a badge on his shirt. "What's happening here?" he asked.

"A wedding party."

"Anyone there a doctor?"

"None for miles."

"That's too bad. I got a sick man in the wagon." He waved the lantern back across the wagon, and light spilled across the bed and a man lying in it. McCan drew in his breath.

It was Evan Bridger.

PART IV

THE LAST DAYS

CHAPTER 26

"My name is Taylor Longhurst," the man with the badge said to the huddle of people who gathered around Bridger's unconscious form. "I'm a U.S. deputy marshal out of Fort Maginnis. That man is Evan Bridger. He's my prisoner."

"Bridger?" someone said. "I've heard of him. Old highwayman and stock rustler."

"That and more," Longhurst said. "He also was the thief once of an army payroll, which makes him of interest to the federal government. That's why I've got him."

McCan asked, "What's wrong with him?"

"I think a recurrence of malaria. I'd bet this old bird came across the isthmus in '49 or so."

Bridger had been found, Longhurst said, passed out in the back of a one-room saloon at a one-horse settlement to the southwest. The saloon owner saw Longhurst's badge and called him in. Longhurst recognized Bridger, and for a day had been seeking medical help for him.

"We've got no doctor," Upchurch said, "but I'll send to Milestown for one right now. There's a small apartment in the back of the store, and you can keep him there."

"No jail?"

"We're a new community."

"The store it is, then. I'm obliged."

They placed Bridger on a cot. When the others were gone, McCan lingered to talk to Longhurst.

"I know Bridger," he said. "At least, I've had encounters with him going back several years. I met him first in Deadwood, down in Dakota."

"Where did you see him last?"

McCan paused, then decided to tell the truth. "At a shooting match between some cattlemen and rustlers. I was with the former, and him the latter."

"I see." Longhurst looked like he knew more than he was saying. "Vigilantism isn't legal, you know. But it isn't easily stopped." He smiled vaguely. "Sometimes it isn't a thing we see much need to interfere in."

McCan relaxed. "This time it turned into something it wasn't supposed to be."

"So I heard. And Bridger was there, Mister . . ."

"McCan. Call me Luke. Yes, he was there."

Longhurst took out a snuff tin and delicately placed a pinch of the powdered tobacco on his thumb. He snorted it up his long nose with a satisfied wince. He offered some to McCan, who declined.

"Can't live without the stuff myself," Longhurst said. "Listen, I could use some sleep. I like the look of you. Are you needing a job?"

"It so happens . . ."

"You got one. Consider yourself deputized. You guard Bridger, and I'll see you get good compensation for it. It should be easy. He ain't going anywhere, sick as he is."

Longhurst gave McCan a shotgun with sawed-off barrels and put him in a chair by the door of the little apartment. The lawman went to the other side of the store, threw together a pile of empty feed sacks, tossed a blanket over them, and went to sleep.

McCan studied Bridger. The outlaw looked terrible, almost dead. *Looks like you may get that justice you always wanted yet, Caleb,* McCan thought.

An hour later Upchurch came in. He approached and looked at Bridger a few moments.

"I figured you'd be off on your wedding trip," McCan said.

"No trip for now. Too much work. And now this outlaw's here, there's even more reason to stay."

"Shouldn't you be with your bride?"

"She's who sent me in here. The thought of this man scares her. I think maybe it reminds her of the night her father died. Have you heard that story? A man like this one broke into her home. Her father and another cowboy came and—"

"I've heard," McCan said. He felt sullen; Maggie obviously had never told Upchurch who that other cowboy had been.

"Why are *you* here?" Upchurch asked.

"I'm deputized."

"I see." Upchurch turned away. "Well, I'll leave you to your work." He headed for the door.

"Upchurch."

"Yes?"

"Congratulations. Take good care of her."

"Thank you. I will." He went out the door and locked it behind him.

After a time, McCan became sleepy, so he went to the wood stove in the middle of the store, built a fire, and made coffee. He drank cup after cup of it until dawn. Longhurst stirred awake, stretched, and went for a cup himself. He came back with it and leaned against the apartment doorframe, his hair disheveled and face whiskered.

"How's our prisoner?" he said.

"Didn't move all night."

"This old bird's going to kick, I believe." Longhurst took a sip of coffee and made a face. "Tastes like a horse peed in this."

"I did my best. I'm worn out. Can I take off now?"

"Go ahead," the lawman said. "Get some rest and come back about supper time. I'll be needing a night guard until he's ready to ride. Or dead."

"I got a friend who could use a job too . . ."

"Is he reliable?"

"Absolutely."

"I got me a day guard then. Send him on."

As McCan left, Longhurst went through a snort-and-sniff routine with his snuff. McCan rode out to the little house, found Bill, and told him about the job.

"I don't know," Bill said. "Bridger killed my brother's murderer. I owe him a debt for that."

But finally he relented, for he needed the job badly. He rode to the Emporium, and McCan crawled into bed.

When McCan returned to the store about dusk, Bill was there with the shotgun in his lap. Longhurst sat on a cracker barrel, eating pickles and drinking warm beer.

"Did that doctor get in?" McCan asked.

"Nope. But we found an old Union medic who checked him out. Bridger's going to be sick for days."

McCan went to Bill. "You been sitting all day?"

"Yep."

"Doesn't Longhurst do any guarding himself?"

"Nope." He smiled.

"Lazy lawman, huh?"

Longhurst called, "You two are doing a good job. Proud of you." He drew more snuff up his nose, then expelled it in a loud sneeze.

At the sound, Bridger opened his eyes. He focused on McCan, then was out again.

CHAPTER 27

Over the next several days, Bridger became first an attraction for visitors, then a fixture that drew little attention. Awareness came slowly to him, strength even slower. He recognized McCan, and was amused their paths had crossed yet again.

"You and me seem bound to run into each other," Bridger said. "By the way, I almost blew off your head at the Breaks before I recognized you."

"I'm obliged you didn't."

"Then let me go."

"I can't do that."

Bridger laughed. "A man can do whatever he wants. Once you figure that out, it frees you up considerable."

"You're not very free right now."

"Freer than men who spend their lives with codes and rules. I never could tolerate that."

"So you don't believe in rules?"

"I don't believe in good or bad, right or wrong, God above or devil below. I believe in Evan Bridger."

"So what kept you from killing me?"

"I didn't feel the urge. Maybe I like your face."

"What do you think of me now, guarding you with a shotgun?"

Bridger shrugged. "You're doing a job. Nothing personal."

McCan leaned back in his chair. "You're right about one thing—we have had a bunch of encounters through the years. Same with me and Caleb Black. He just turns up. Or used to. I think he's dead. You can rest easier now, I reckon."

Bridger looked at the ceiling, mulling over the information. "Why do you think he's dead?"

"I was with him this year when we got jumped in camp. There was shooting. I got away, but we got separated. I never found him, but there was sign he had died."

Bridger smiled. "So, old Caleb's killed! I wish it could have been me that done it."

McCan's temper flared. "Caleb was my friend. God knows it would have been better for a lousy child-killer like you to have died instead of him."

Bridger's smile vanished. "What did you call me?"

McCan was silent.

"I never killed no child."

"You just don't know you did."

Bridger's smile slowly returned. "You're joshing with me. Trying to get me riled."

"I don't know why being called a child-killer would rile a man who doesn't believe in right or wrong."

"You don't think too highly of me, do you?" Bridger said. "How much do you know about me, about who I really am?"

"Not much."

"Let me give you some history. I was born in Baltimore, in an alley by a church where folks in fancy clothes sang hymns while drunks froze to death at the back door. I never knew my father, nor my mother, except that she was a whore who left me in a pile of rags at a stable door. I never had even the first suck at her breast. A policeman found me. I was raised in an orphanage six years, fighting and scrapping with the others, and never crying my first tear. I ain't cried it yet.

"They finally shipped me off to a preacher, who kept me for nine hard years. He preached at me, screamed at me, beat me, told me the meek would inherit the earth and I'd better get meek, by God. But I knew about his drinking, and the way he beat his woman and run around on her with a darky girl across town. I hated that man. When I ran off, I left his house burning, and I hope it cooked him.

"I stole, rolled drunks and such to live, and worked my way west to Kansas. When I was full-growed, I married a gal and ran a little farm, until she died having a baby. I buried them both. Killed a man the next night in a card game—he cheated, but it was really out of grief that I done it.

"I went to California during the rush—picked up this sickness on the way—and mined until I figured out it was easier to steal gold than grub it. Since then, I've been most everywhere, doing what I want. That's the way it'll be with me until I'm dead—doing what I want. If that's good or bad, I don't give a damn. That, son, is who Evan Bridger is: a man who just don't give a damn."

Bridger stopped talking. McCan said, "I'm grateful to you for helping me in Deadwood, and for not killing me up on the Missouri Breaks. But the fact is, the world will be a better place the day you go in the ground, and the air will be a little cleaner the day you quit breathing it."

Bridger laughed. He was tired, and closed his eyes. For several minutes he seemed to be asleep, but then he looked again at McCan and asked, "Why did you call me a child-killer?"

"Caleb Black's wife was pregnant when you killed her. Not that you give a damn."

Bridger's lip twitched almost imperceptibly. "Yeah," he said, and closed his eyes again.

McCan stood guard the next night, and this time Bridger did not talk. He was worse, his fever higher, his eyes sunken deeper.

In the silence, McCan dozed, the shotgun across his lap. Something made him wake up an hour later. He looked groggily at a figure before him in the flaring lamplight.

"Good to see you, Luke."

McCan blinked to be sure he was awake—he was. "Good to see you too Caleb. I thought you were dead."

"I thought *you* were dead. How'd you get away?"

"I knocked out the one after me and hid out in the woods until morning. How about you?"

"Me and the other took a shot from each other. His was worse. I passed out in the woods for about a day. I think he died by the river and fell in."

Black turned to Bridger, who was asleep. "Would he have lived?"

"What do you mean, 'would'?"

"I mean, would he have lived if I hadn't showed up, because I'm going to kill him right here."

McCan raised his shotgun. Black looked at him like he was insane.

"What are you doing?" Black demanded.

"Stopping you, it appears."

"Why?"

"I don't know. It's my job."

Black glared disbelievingly at him. "I ought to shoot *you*."

"You'd shoot me just to get him?"

"You turned saint or something, Luke?"

"Not saint. Just deputy."

In Black's mind, a game of balancing, debating, option-shifting went on. It evidenced itself in subtle movements of his fingers near his side arm. Black was coiled tight, ready to be sprung with a breath. But, after several tense moments, he relaxed. The fingers went still.

"I'll get my chance," he said. "They'll never get him to no prison. I'll get to him first."

"I don't doubt it. It just won't be tonight."

"Maybe we'll run across each other again, Luke."

"I don't doubt that, either."

Black walked out. Bridger moaned and stirred. He sweated profusely. McCan gripped his shotgun so tightly his fingers were numb. He, too, sweated.

The door of the Emporium, its lock ruined by Caleb's entry, banged shut. Black was gone. All was silent except Bridger's labored breathing, which rattled like a tinker's wagon, and the buzzing of a fly trapped in a web in some dark corner of the store.

CHAPTER 28

When Bill Webster relieved McCan the next morning, he came in late and noticeably happier than before.

"I got a new job," he announced. "Over at the LU Bar, starting as soon as I can get there."

"Good," McCan said. "Are you healed up enough to do it?"

"These bones ache a bit, but a man can't let that stop him."

"Nope." He slapped Bill's shoulder. "When will you go?"

"Tomorrow morning. Maybe Longhurst can find somebody else to sit day guard."

McCan went to the porch of the store and rolled a cigarette. Upchurch came around the corner as Longhurst rode in from the north. He had abandoned his feed-sack bed in the store for a real one in a spare room at a ranch three miles away. McCan nodded his usual silent greeting at Upchurch and waited until Longhurst had dismounted.

"Looks like you'll have to do some guarding yourself," he said. "Bill Webster won't be around starting tomorrow."

Upchurch, who saw the damaged lock on the door, turned to McCan. "What happened to this?"

McCan debated: tell the truth? He decided against it. "I caught somebody trying to get in last night," he said. "I ran them off, but they already had busted the lock."

Upchurch looked worried. "Thieves!" he exclaimed, as if the thought was novel. "Thank you for running them off. Did you see their faces?"

"Too dark."

Longhurst asked, "Why is Bill leaving?"

McCan told him about the new job. "I'll just take his place myself, then," Longhurst said, looking glum.

"No," Upchurch said. "I'll do it."

McCan was surprised. "But you've got a store to run!"

"If my store is threatened by thieves, I want people to become used to seeing me with a shotgun in my lap. That might deter any other attempts like this one."

Have mercy, McCan thought. *Rodney Upchurch, deputy. The daisy-plucker of law enforcement.*

Longhurst, seeing a chance to preserve his cherished idleness, immediately accepted Upchurch's offer. "Excellent suggestion," he said. "Do you have any experience with shotguns?"

"None beyond selling them."

Longhurst took the shotgun from McCan and dug extra shells from his saddlebag. "Come on. I'll give you some lessons."

McCan went back to his chair at Bridger's door to stand guard until they were through. Moments later, the shotgun boomed off behind the building. Bridger jerked up with a choked cry in the back of his throat.

"Don't worry," McCan said. "Nobody's shooting at you. Yet."

Upchurch apparently enjoyed guard duty. As Bridger improved again over the next few days, Upchurch befriended him. Whenever McCan came to relieve Upchurch, merchant and outlaw were always deep in conversation.

But Bridger had little to say to McCan anymore. When McCan was with him, he either slept or just stared at the ceiling. If McCan asked a question, Bridger merely shrugged or muttered something vague in response.

Still, Bridger's health was obviously returning, Longhurst often came in to evaluate his prisoner, and at length told McCan he would be well enough for travel soon. "I want you to go with me," Longhurst said. "An extra guard would be helpful."

The day before they were to leave for Fort Maginnis, McCan passed the shotgun to Upchurch, as usual, and went off to bed. He was restless today, though, and spent most of the morning puttering about. Finally, about noon, he went back to his bunk and fell asleep.

He awoke later than usual. Darkness was heavy. He intuitively felt something was wrong back at the Emporium.

He rode to it at a gallop, throat tight, a sheen of dampness on his forehead, though the night was cool. At the store, all was in commotion—men moving about, more lights than usual, a jumble of loud voices.

He dismounted and hitched his horse. "What happened?" he asked a man standing nearby.

"Mr. Upchurch has been shot," the man said.

McCan pushed through the crowd into the store.

Longhurst was there, his usual half-cocky smile gone, his face gray as coal ash.

"How'd it happen?"

"Bridger somehow just got the shotgun and used it," Longhurst said. "Shot Upchurch in the side, and him unarmed."

"Is he dead?"

"No. But he's bad—his side looks like chewed meat."

Maggie. McCan had to see her.

He circled the store to the house behind it; even more people were there. He entered the main room.

The bedroom door stood ajar. Upchurch lay in there, bloodied and pale, his eyes squeezed shut, his breathing spasmodic. Somebody worked on him, digging out pellets from his mangled side.

McCan looked for Maggie but did not see her. He left the house.

He found her around back, crying. He said nothing, just stood holding his hat and wondering if he should slip away and leave her alone. But suddenly she became aware of him. She came into his arms and wept against his shoulder. When the crying was finished, she looked into his face.

"Find that man, Luke. Find him and bring him back—or kill him. He's taken my husband from me."

"I will, Maggie. And your husband will be all right. A lot of good folks here are taking care of him."

He led Maggie to the back step and made her sit, then went inside and got coffee. "Drink this," he said. "It will help."

McCan sought out Longhurst again. "When do we ride?"

"First light. Bridger stole a horse, and he'll have a good lead. I figure he'll steal another one as soon as he can. I just hope nobody else gets shot."

"Will you organize a full posse?"

"No. Just you and me. It will be quieter and quicker that way. We'll catch that bird. We'll bring him back for trial."

Not if I make the choice, McCan thought. *If it's up to me, we'll bring him back dead.*

CHAPTER 29

Standing before his hovel of a house, a skinny man old and shriveled from sun—wiped his hands across his mouth and said, "He was here, all right. Came riding in all a-lather and aimed a shotgun at my belly. 'Give me a horse,' he says, and I did. He was a ghastly soul, all pasty and sweaty. I done like he said."

"You did right," Longhurst said. "He would have killed you if you hadn't, and you're lucky he didn't anyway. Which way did he go?"

"West. And that's a funny thing—he said where he was going, and to make sure whoever followed him knew."

"Trying to bluff us off his trail, probably," Longhurst said. "What did he say?"

"Garrison's, over on Froze To Death Creek."

McCan said, "I know the place. Just a lonely old outpost."

Longhurst crossed his arms on his saddle horn and looked thoughtful. "The odds are he was lying, but we've got little chance to catch him at any rate. Maybe we ought to follow the only clue we've got."

"What are you suggesting?"

"Take Bridger at his word. Go to Garrison's."

They tipped hats to the old man and rode away, heading due west. McCan was amazed to see Longhurst successfully take a double load of snuff while riding in a good breeze and not lose a grain.

"How long you been snorting that stuff?" McCan asked.

"Since I was six. I got only one regret about it, and that's that I didn't start when I was five."

They rode steadily, following a trail here, a wagon road there. Each had brought an extra horse, and they changed periodically to keep the animals fresh.

To McCan, there was something ironic in the situation: here he was, tracking the outlaw Caleb Black had sought for years, one who had brought pain to a lady he cared about, one who deserved death if any man did. And this after McCan had protected that same outlaw from his deserved fate only shortly before.

He couldn't forget that if he had let Black kill Bridger there in the Emporium, Maggie would not be in the torment she now was.

They pushed steadily and ate up another twenty-five miles before dark. Longhurst built a fire, cooked beans and bacon, and brewed coffee. McCan was on his second cup when Longhurst grinned.

"That Arbuckle has a special ingredient."

"No."

"Yes."

Longhurst laughed, lay down, and almost immediately began snoring. McCan shook his head. Probably the laziest, most devil-may-care deputy in the hire of the government, yet he had to like him. He even liked the snuff-tainted coffee he brewed.

The next day they cut southwest and marked off thirty hard miles, camping near Great Porcupine Creek. McCan was bone-weary and rump-sore from the saddle. Manhunting was as hard on a man as roundup. Harder, for there was a gnawing uncertainty about what would happen at the end.

The next day they rose before dawn and ate a quick breakfast of jerky strips. They rode hard, for today they would reach the trading post where Bridger had said he would go.

McCan and Longhurst sat mounted at the base of a slate-colored slope, looking up through a forest of pine and elder, studying the nondescript trading post called Garrison's.

"Think he's there?" McCan asked.

"Depends on how sick he was when he relieved that old man of his horse. He might not have been clearheaded enough to lie."

"Well, let's ride in and see."

They tied their mounts at a water trough at the front of the post, unbooted their rifles, and walked into the largest of the three log buildings comprising Garrison's. The air was close inside, very dank, smelling of rot and other foul things. At a long bar of puncheon boards laid out on stumps was a fortyish man with one ear. He was, McCan assumed, the barkeep, but, from the look of him, might be a whiskey-runner or Indian trader.

There were others too. Three men shoveled beans into their mouths at a corner table. Another sat alone in the back, drinking. His face was turned to the wall; for a moment, McCan thought it was Bridger, but it wasn't.

Longhurst went to the bar and ordered two glasses of whiskey. McCan sipped his; it tasted like a mix of brimstone and alcohol. He made a face. "Don't drop an ash into this, Longhurst. It would flare in your face."

He did not notice the movement of one of the men at the table at his mention of the deputy's name.

Longhurst did notice. He watched the man out of the corner of his eye as he drained the liquor in one swallow. He smacked his lips and shook his head. "Sweet as candy." He clicked his glass against the bar for a refill, and shifted position to allow a casual but more direct look at the bean-eaters. He took a snort of snuff as he eyed them.

McCan realized what was happening, and also that Longhurst had left his badge on his shirt. He wished he had taken it off.

Longhurst sipped his second glassful rather than gulped it. One of the men at the table stood and walked toward him and McCan.

Longhurst grinned. "Well, howdy, Grunt! Long time no see. How's that hand?"

McCan pieced it together quickly. This man apparently was one of Longhurst's old captures. The reference to the hand he interpreted after a glance at the man's mangled right extremity. Something had pulverized it long ago—a sawed-off shotgun, maybe?

"I wondered when I'd see you again, Longhurst."

"When did they let you out, Grunt? I thought you'd be in a lot longer than this."

"Things have a way of working out." The man smiled, revealing teeth moldier than a swamp log.

Longhurst took another sip. "Can I buy you a drink? You'd like this stuff, Grunt—tastes like it was drained out of a hell-pit. A man's drink for sure."

"Why are you here, lawman?"

"Just out doing my job. Grunt, it's coming back to me—seems I heard you escaped."

"What do you plan to do about it?"

"Well, I'm in a good humor. I'd like to cut a deal. I won't arrest you if you'll give me some information about the man I'm looking for."

"Arrest?" Grunt laughed. "Hear that, boys? He said he'd not *arrest* me. Longhurst, I got grave doubts you'll ever arrest anybody again!"

This time Longhurst laughed. He nudged McCan. "Hear that, Luke? He said *grave*."

Something in the air snapped. Grunt lunged for his pistol, but Longhurst was ready. He drew easily and fired twice. Grunt's ugly face twisted and he fell back, screaming. Blood spurted from what had been his un-mangled left hand—now missing a thumb and forefinger.

One of the men with Grunt ran out the front door, arms outstretched, body careening. The second looked momentarily as if he might join the fight, but Longhurst turned his pistol on him and the man slipped sideways, then bolted for the door. Grunt, still yelling and gripping his bloody hand with the shotgun-mangled paw that was his other, quickly followed.

"That boy'll have to quit messing with me, or eventually he won't even be able to pick his nose," Longhurst said.

Suddenly the deputy screamed. He had rested his left arm on the bartop, and now he pulled it around in front of him. Blood dripped from it. Behind Longhurst, the barkeep drew up the Bowie he had used to gash the arm. It came arcing down, and McCan yelled and threw out his own arm to block it.

That saved Longhurst from taking a full-blade stab in the back, but the knife went in four inches at least, and Longhurst screamed once more.

McCan went for his pistol, but the lone man who had been drinking in the back made that unnecessary.

The man rose, turned, adeptly fired. The barkeep gave a thoroughly canine bark and fell sideways to the floor. He grasped his wounded left arm, and the knife fell from his hand. McCan kicked it away.

"Oh lordy, oh lordy, oh lordy," Longhurst said, over and over again, falling on his knees so the chant became a strange parody of prayer. "Oh lordy, oh lordy, oh lordy."

McCan turned from him to the man in the back, then slumped against the bar, shaking his head.

"I should have guessed I'd run into you, Caleb."

Caleb Black smiled. "Why not? We're two hounds chasing the same rabbit."

He crossed the room and shook McCan's hand. Longhurst quit his chant and started moaning, and the wounded barkeep did too. It made an eerie barnyard harmony: the barkeep howling like a kicked beagle, the lawman whining like a cat.

CHAPTER 30

McCan went to the writhing barkeep and knelt to touch the man's injured arm. The barkeep rolled onto his back and looked at McCan, who only now recognized him.

"You don't hold a grudge, do you, Luke? You don't hold a grudge after all these years?" the man whined.

McCan was momentarily too surprised to speak. The barkeep took that for a bad sign and howled out again, a sort of coward's deathsong.

"Oh, shut up, Sturley," McCan said. "I don't figure to kill you, though it'd be a loss to nobody if I did."

Roy Sturley hushed. "Thank you, Luke. God bless you, son. I always thought the highest of you, I really did."

"How'd you lose that ear?"

"It was bit off in a fight."

"Good for whoever. You know there was a time I was set on killing you, Roy?"

"I ain't surprised, Luke. I didn't always do right by you, but we're friends now—huh?"

"You'll never be that, but I'm letting you off just the same. Now tell me why you cut my partner."

"I seen he was a lawman, and that he was with you, and thought maybe he was after me. I'm sorry, honest I am."

Longhurst was angry. He stood and wheeled toward the prone man. "Give me a reason I shouldn't gut you like a hog right here!"

Sturley scooted away on his back until he was against the wall, anticipating his own slaughter.

"Leave him be, Longhurst. He might help us," McCan said. To Sturley he said, "You remember the night Jimmy Wyatt got killed? The man who did it was Evan Bridger. We're looking for him. Have you seen him here?"

Sturley said, "There was a man on a lame horse, wanting a trade. I didn't have nothing for him, so he went on. It might have been Evan Bridger, but I don't know for sure because I wasn't there to see who shot Jimmy."

"That's right—you ran off. You were as big a coward then as now," McCan said.

"This fellow, what did he look like?" Black asked.

"Tall, pepper-haired, skin kind of loose—like he'd lost weight—and he looked sickly."

"And he's on a lame horse?"

"That's right, sir."

"He'll have stole or traded for another by now," Longhurst said. He thrust his hand out to Black. "Taylor Longhurst. Thanks for your help."

"I'm Caleb Black." The men shook. "Luke's an old friend of mine. We've got a way of running into each other every now and then."

"Seems I've heard about a Caleb Black who trails Evan Bridger."

"I'm the man," Black said. "Though I'm no ghost, despite what a few say."

"I thought you were a story somebody made up."

"Bridger wishes I was."

McCan shook Sturley by the shoulder. Sturley's face screwed up like a crumpled mask. "What else do you know?" McCan demanded.

"A letter. He left a letter and said, give it to any lawman who came after him."

"A *letter?* Where?"

Sturley pointed to a folded piece of paper sticking out from a crevice in the wall behind the bar. Black took it, opened it, and read.

"It's just a note," he said. "It says, 'To you on my trail, find C. Black and tell him the game is over and it is time to settle and he'll know the place if he is savvy. E. Bridger.' " Black refolded the paper, frowning.

"What does *that* mean?" McCan asked.

"I don't know," Black said. "It's mighty strange. He's never done nothing like this before."

McCan looked again at Sturley. "Did he say where he was going?"

"Billings. He said to be sure and tell he was going straight to Billings."

"First time I've ever had a criminal tell me where I could catch him," Longhurst said, his voice stressed from pain.

McCan looked at Sturley's wound. "I'll bind that up for you," he said. "The bullet went clean through, so you'll be all right. Which proves there's no justice: you live, and Bob Webster died."

When McCan was finished, Sturley struggled to his feet, slid in his own blood, and fell. He scrambled up again and rushed out the door.

"I'm hurting bad," Longhurst said. "That blade was hot as a brand."

"I'm no doc, but Luke can tell you I'm a fair nurse-maid when I got to be," Black said. "Let me see what I can do for you."

Longhurst took off his shirt and sat on a bench. Black poured whiskey across his bleeding back, and onto the sliced arm. Longhurst yelled and almost passed out.

"Give me some of that," he said. He grabbed the bottle and took a long swallow. Then he snorted a pile of snuff into his sinuses and seemed to feel better.

"Let's get out of here," McCan said. "This blood is drawing flies. Taylor, I take it that Grunt fellow was an old friend of yours."

"One of many," the deputy said.

Longhurst became sick that night. His pain worsened, and he threw up his supper right after he ate it. He lay on his bedroll somewhere between wakefulness and stupor.

"He can't go on," McCan said to Black.

"That's no good," Black said. "We're so close to Bridger I can smell him."

"We won't lose him," McCan said. "He's marked his trail from the beginning. I don't understand it, but it's like he wants to be caught."

"Something's different, that's for sure. The letter alone proves that." Black borrowed McCan's makings and rolled a smoke. "All right," he said. "I'll help you find a place to let the lawman heal a little. But after that, I'm going on, with or without you."

Five miles beyond Muggins Creek the next day, they found a humble spread wedged into a shallow valley. It was small, poorly built, impoverished. Some cowpoke's attempt to build a cattle operation of his own, McCan guessed. If so, his success was meager. A few scrawny cattle ranged within view, along with a couple of horses and a yardful of chickens. Only a vegetable patch appeared to be thriving.

"Let's go in," McCan said. He rode toward the house. Behind him, Longhurst trailed along, his face flushed and wet. Black rode in the rear, looking about thoughtfully.

"Hello, the house!" McCan shouted. "Anybody here?"

No one answered. Only the chickens responded, clucking and bustling away. McCan dismounted some distance from the house and walked in.

"Hello!" he shouted again. He went to the door and knocked.

Something moved inside. He rapped again, gave another hello, then stepped back. A moment later the latch moved, and the door opened about halfway. A boy appeared, his brows and mouth quirked downward in a scowl. He held an ancient percussion cap revolver.

"Oh," McCan said. "I didn't mean to trespass."

"What's your business, mister?" Illogically, the voice surprised McCan. The dark little face could have been that of an old man, but the voice was merely the elfin squeak of a very scared boy.

"My name is McCan. I've got a friend out here, a deputy territorial marshal, who was hurt by a criminal. He was stabbed and he's sick. We hoped you'd let us lay him up here for a bit."

At mention of the lawman, the boy looked confused. The expression, though, evolved quickly into one of resolute inapproachability. "We got no place here," the boy said. "You can ride on."

"All right then. Where's the next spread?"

"Twenty miles west. Or you can get to Junction City, due south. It's closer."

"Thank you. I'm leaving, and I'd appreciate you being real careful with that hogleg." McCan returned to the horses, shrugging.

"I can't believe it," Black said. "It ain't typical of these parts to turn somebody away needing help."

"I wasn't about to push him, not with that pistol in his hand. We'd best head for Junction City."

They turned mounts and rode away, but Caleb Black raised his hand and they stopped. "Look yonder," he said. He pointed toward the horses grazing nearby. One was a scrawny black mare. But the other was a gray gelding with a bad leg.

McCan didn't grasp the significance at first, but suddenly he remembered: Sturley had said Bridger was on a lame horse.

"Just keep calm and ride off like nothing's happened," Black instructed. "Once we clear the ridge, we'll cut around and wait for dark. Then we can slip in. Taylor, you can rest it out on your bedroll."

A few minutes later they stopped, hidden beyond the rise. Longhurst found a shady spot and laid down, complaining about dizziness and pain.

"No wonder the boy acted so funny, if Bridger really is in there," McCan said. "I had a peculiar feeling the whole time I was at that door."

Black checked his pistol. "I'm bellying up to where I can see the house. If he slips out, I want to know it."

McCan went with him, and they laid on their stomachs and watched the little building. No one emerged for a long time, and when finally the door opened, only the boy came out. He went to a shed, came back with a hoe, and went to work in the vegetable patch.

When it was nearly dark, the boy went back inside. McCan and Black slid, silent as the moonlight, across the clearing to the door. They drew their pistols and readied themselves on either side of the doorway; then Black wheeled and kicked the door open.

He and McCan rushed in and leveled their pistols on the occupants.

There were only two of them. The boy, gaping, and a lady, who had once been pretty but now looked faded—somehow eroded. Evan Bridger was not there.

The lady cried out and rushed to her boy. She hugged him close, protectively. McCan saw the broad swell of her belly. She was pregnant.

Black lowered his pistol and thumbed down the hammer. His face was deathly pale. "My god," he murmured. "I almost shot her."

For a moment, McCan thought Black was going to pass out.

CHAPTER 31

Her name was Jerusha Harpe, and for more than eight months she had lived with one child struggling to survive inside her, another struggling to survive without. She tried at first to make the intruders believe her husband would quickly be home, but it was soon evident she was lying. When her fright faded and reassurance came after they brought in Taylor Longhurst and showed his badge, she admitted her husband was dead.

"We're sorry," McCan said. "About that, and how we busted in here. We thought a very dangerous man was in here with you."

"There *was* a man here," she said. "But he was gone long before you came. He said men were after him, and there was someplace he had to go, where—what was it he said, George?"

"Where it all could end," the boy said. His face no longer tight with fear, he looked like a child again.

"Yes. Where it all could end. I didn't understand what that meant. He was strange. Like he was losing his sanity."

"I can believe it," Black said.

"But he was tender, in one way," she continued. "Particularly toward me, even though he held his pistol in his hand the whole time he was here—maybe six or seven hours. Most of what he said made no sense. And he just kept staring at my—" She became embarrassed. She glanced down and touched her protruding belly.

Black said, "Something's happening to him. Messages to us, him asking for me to be brought into the search—I don't understand this."

"I was afraid when you came," Jerusha said. "That's why I had George stand you off at the door. I didn't know who you were, or if you might not be just as dangerous as that man was. You know, he never said his name."

"His name is Evan Bridger," McCan said. "Have you heard of him?"

Jerusha shook her head, but the boy nodded excitedly. "I know—he's an outlaw. A robber and a killer. And he's haunted by a ghost that stays on his trail and tries to kill *him*."

"Don't talk nonsense, George," Jerusha scolded. "People tell all kinds of silly stories."

McCan looked at Black, who seemed not to have heard. He was thinking, apparently very seriously. And he, like Bridger had done, stared at Jerusha's pregnant belly.

"That story's *true*, Ma!" George said. "Everybody tells it. I wish Pa could know I'd met a real outlaw!"

Jerusha frowned; the lines around her eyes became more evident. "If your pa was here, this outlaw never would have come in on us. And besides that, your pa wouldn't have thought much of you being pleased to have met such an evil man. If this Evan Bridger is evil, then I can tell you it's no ghost that haunts him, but something else. You remember what I've read to you about the wicked?"

George Harpe twisted his mouth and plucked a scripture verse from his memory: " 'The wicked flee when no man pursueth.' "

"That's right," Jerusha said. "What chases them? Their own conscience. Knowledge of their own evil."

McCan stood, digging for his makings. "Not in Bridger's case, ma'am. The man's got no conscience. He doesn't believe in good or bad—told me so himself. There is no evil as far as he's concerned."

Jerusha gave McCan a stern look, and he saw she did not appreciate being contradicted in front of her son. "There is not a man who has walked this earth who doesn't have to face his own evil at some point. There's not a man who can deny it forever," she said.

McCan was sheepish. "Yes, ma'am. I'm sorry. I'll just step out for a smoke now."

He went outside and lit up. The rich smoke kicked pleasantly against the back of his throat. He walked around the little spread and wondered how a pregnant widow and a twelve-year-old boy managed to survive here.

Inside, Caleb Black was still lost in thought. He didn't notice when Jerusha Harpe rose heavily from her chair and walked stiff-legged to the stove. She brewed coffee and brought a cup to Black. She thrust it before his eyes, and he looked up and smiled at her.

In the corner, Taylor Longhurst moaned and twisted on a cot.

"God have mercy on a knife-stuck sinner," he said.

George Harpe bounded to his side. "Are you hurting, mister?"

"Yes. And out of snuff. Be a good boy and head to the shed where my saddlebags are. There's some inside there."

The boy ran out the door, proud of his assignment. He darted past McCan, into the shed, and came out again with Longhurst's snuff in hand. McCan touched his shoulder and stopped him.

"How long until your mother's to give birth, George?"

"Any day now. That's what the granny woman says."

"Where does the granny woman live?"

"Down toward Junction City. About five miles from here."

McCan nodded and blew smoke through his nostrils. "Maybe it's providential we came by when we did, then. Your ma might need help real soon."

A peal of thunder grumbled across the sky. McCan breathed deeply and tasted a hint of distant rain.

"We're in for a storm," he said.

McCan's predictions were correct. The rain came at dark, the baby at midnight.

McCan rode off with directions from George, hoping he could find the midwife's house, praying he could get back with her in time. He left Caleb Black with Jerusha, Caleb's hands scrubbed clean and his shirt stripped off, ready to do what he could if the child came quickly.

The storm whipped McCan without mercy. Rain slapped him like hail, stinging his face and lips. Lightning ripped jagged tears through the night, spooking his horse, but also providing the only light by which he could keep to the road.

The wind blew against him, and progress was slow. By the time he reached the dirt-roofed hovel where the midwife lived, he feared he was too late. Jerusha's labor had come swiftly and hard, and by now the baby surely had been born. Or lost.

The midwife was old, but moved nimbly. She wrapped a heavy shawl around her shoulders and mounted behind McCan, her fat-dangling arms around his waist. McCan spurred his tired mount back the way it had come.

The storm abated when they were halfway home, and when they reached the Harpe cabin, the sky was clear. McCan slid down and helped the midwife descend, then whipped his still-saddled mount into the corral. He trotted to the house, threw open the door, and went to the bedroom.

He stopped, overwhelmed by what he saw.

Caleb stood beside Jerusha's bed, his skin slicked with sweat and golden in the lamplight. He beamed, face upturned, as he lifted a tiny, red, squalling girl who barely filled his broad hands.

The infant, shining with its mother's water and blood, cried in hoarse, steady bursts. Caleb Black laughed at the sound, and when he laid the child into the upheld arms of its mother, Jerusha laughed too.

CHAPTER 32

Days passed, and Caleb said nothing about going after Bridger. Instead, he took care of the new mother, and when Caleb—big, gruff, bearded—cradled the child in his burly forearms, it reminded McCan of a pink baby robin nested in an ancient, battered oak. The man and child played a delightful counterpoint to each other.

Jerusha named the girl Lucy, after her grandmother. Lucy was a scrappy, healthy infant who thrived at her mother's breast, and it was clear she was deeply loved by the man who had first held her.

Longhurst, meanwhile, recovered from his wounds, fighting off an infection that had set into his arm. He grew restless to move on. McCan, too, knew that the longer they waited, the less likely they were to catch Bridger.

Bridger had indicated he was going to Billings, but that had been days ago. They needed to ride at once. Ironically, it was Black who was the least concerned. He was preoccupied with Jerusha and Lucy and George.

Longhurst called aside his two partners and said, "It's time to go. We need to ride out at first light tomorrow."

McCan nodded, but Black looked displeased. "We owe it to Jerusha to make sure she's in fit shape before we leave," he said.

"She's in fine shape already, and we've paid our obligation to her a dozen times over—you especially, Caleb. Now, I'm going on tomorrow, and if you want to come, you're welcome. If not, it'll just be me and Luke—or maybe just me." He looked inquiringly at McCan.

"I'll be along," McCan said.

Black fidgeted, but finally he nodded. "First light, then."

George waved them out of sight the next morning. Black would not look back at him. McCan watched his old partner thoughtfully, and while Longhurst was ahead, came to Black's side.

"You think highly of this family."

Black smiled. "I've surprised myself, Luke. It's the first time in years I haven't been jumping to go after Bridger. That's been my whole life up until now."

"And now?"

"Now I just don't know. Nothing makes sense. When I caught that baby, it was like it would have been if Annie hadn't been killed and things had gone on like they should. I got a glimpse of what it would be to really have a life again."

McCan said, "Have all these years of chasing an outlaw and living on the trail been a waste then?"

Black thought a few moments before he answered. "For a man to waste his life, he's got to have one to waste. I never did. Not after Bridger killed Annie. What was left after that was existence, not life."

"Well, you've got more than that now, Caleb. I saw

you with that baby in your hands. It's a sight I won't forget."

Black spurred on ahead of McCan, ending the conversation. McCan fell back to a comfortable distance and rolled a smoke.

They reached Billings, a little cluster of buildings near the Yellowstone, a few miles above its juncture with Clark Fork. Here they questioned several people, but found no remembrance of Bridger's presence, no clues like those he had left up until now.

"That ends it," Longhurst said. "If he ever was here, he's not now. And there's no way to know where he might have gone. He might even have doubled back on us, or passed us on the other side of a hill."

McCan looked at Black. "Caleb?"

Caleb Black nodded. He was glum, but not furious, as McCan normally would expect. "We've lost his trail," Black said. "And I sure can't guess where he was going."

"He said a place where it could end—a place you would know," McCan said. "That doesn't help?"

Black only shook his head.

Longhurst ingested some snuff and presented his hand. "Gentlemen, it's been fine. I'm sorry we have to end on a failure, but I'm marking this one up to Bridger and heading back to Fort Maginnis. If either of you make it to the South Judith Mountains, I'll expect to see you there."

They shook hands and said their good-byes. McCan and Black watched the deputy ride away whistling, his easy and reckless air utterly undisturbed by the fact that he had lost his prisoner.

"There goes a man who wouldn't care if the sun fizzled out," Black said.

"He'd just figure it a good reason to sleep late," McCan said. "Well, Caleb, what now?"

"I been thinking about a hot bath, in a real tub. A few good cigars, some decent grub—what do you say?"

McCan was agreeable, and the pair checked into a hotel and located a bathhouse. At the latter, they basked in hot, suds-slick water, kept steaming by a fat man with no shirt and no shoes.

McCan said nothing of it, but he detected great levity in Black. He was happy. He joked, smiled— McCan had seen little of that behavior in all the time he had known the man, for from the beginning, Black had struggled with problems ultimately connected to Evan Bridger and his own stubborn pride.

If you had just let it go when Bridger attacked you on the Deadwood Trail, your life would have been a very different one, McCan thought. *But you had to salvage your pride.*

In a little restaurant, they ate fried steak and drank tea. "What's next, Caleb?" McCan asked around the rim of his cup.

"I'm going back to Jerusha and George and Lucy. They could use the help of a man. They're a fine bunch, Luke. I can't stop thinking about them."

"Jerusha in particular?"

Black glanced up, smiling vaguely. "You ain't no cupid, so put away your bow."

"Just talking, that's all."

They ate some more. McCan smoked a cigarette. "What about Bridger?"

"Hell with him."

"You're going to *forget* him?"

"I'm going to try."

McCan slept lightly that night. He listened to Black's snores for two hours before finally falling asleep. Later, he awoke. No snores came from the trundle bed across the room. Black sat on the windowsill, looking at the moon.

"Caleb?"

"Go back to sleep, Luke."

"What's wrong?"

Black shook his head. "I think I know where Bridger went."

"Where?"

"Let's don't talk about it, huh?"

McCan put his hands behind his head. "Will you go back to Jerusha tomorrow?"

There was a long pause. "No. Bridger was right. It's time to end this thing. How could I live with Jerusha, knowing he might show up like he did before, and—" He broke off. "I couldn't stand that again. And I won't put them to the risk."

"I'm going with you."

"No need. It's my fight."

"Not anymore. I made a promise to someone. I plan to keep it."

CHAPTER 33

When McCan awoke in the morning, Black was already up. Whether he had slept or stayed at the window all night, McCan did not know.

McCan splashed water on his face at the basin. "How long until we get there?"

"A few days, pushing hard," Black said.

"Can you tell me where?"

"I don't feel like talking about it. Come along, if you got to."

Black stayed almost completely silent from the time they left Billings. McCan tried to talk to him some, but gave it up, limiting conversation to what was essential and no more. Black was heavyhearted, grim.

The weather cooled dramatically. A heavy breeze whipped down from the western ridges, rustling the conifer groves and making the bunch grass dance. They rode ploddingly, Black always in the lead, but riding as if in no hurry. That, like Black's silence and his unwillingness to talk, puzzled and slightly angered McCan.

They followed the old Bozeman Trail, a cattle route. They went through Bozeman with hardly a pause, following the trail's sharp southward curve toward the Madison River.

As he rode, McCan recalled the night he rode with Jonas Carrington to the house where first he saw Maggie. The memory fit in well with the grimness of the mission and the sense of oppression that exuded from the silent, slumped form of Caleb Black.

They reached Virginia City about noon and stopped for a meal. Black ordered food, then refused to touch it. He stared into a corner while McCan ate and drank and wondered how close they were to the end of it all.

After the meal, they mounted and rode southwest, into the mountains. The air was cool, and in the sky, clouds congealed into a dull spread of flat gray. They rode more than an hour, and at last topped a ridge. There Black stopped, and McCan rode up beside him.

Before them lay a valley, beautiful even in the gloom of this day. A long spine of jagged mountains stretched off to the southwest, rocky and barren at the peaks, dotted with evergreens at the bases. Rich, golden grass grew along the valley bottom where a stream splashed over mossy stones. Willows and elms lined its banks.

Two hundred yards from the stream's widest point, about halfway down the valley, stood a house. It was unpainted, its front built with sawed timbers, its rear with unhewn logs. The front porch roof, supported with cedar poles, sagged in the middle. The door was crumbled and splintered. All about grass, scrub trees, and saplings grew abundantly.

Now McCan understood. "This is your old place, Caleb?"

Black nodded. "Where he killed them."

A roan wandered lazily from the other side of the

house. McCan felt a chill. Bridger *was* here.

"Let's go," Black said.

They rode down slowly, splashing across the stream. A few dozen yards from the house, they dismounted and tied the horses to a sapling.

The door swung open on silent leather hinges, and Bridger stepped onto the porch. The door closed behind him.

Bridger was changed. For one thing, he was drunk— but the change went far beyond that.

He's old, McCan thought. *Ten years older than when I saw him last.*

Bridger wore a Colt. He must have picked it up at Garrison's, maybe even stolen it from Upchurch's Emporium the night he escaped.

"Hello, gentlemen," Bridger slurred. "I've been waiting for you. I didn't know if you'd be savvy enough to trail me here or not." He swept bleary eyes over his old foe. "We've dogged-and-catted it a long time, Caleb."

Black said, "Don't call my name. I don't want it fouled by you."

Bridger laughed. "We ain't led much of a life, either one of us, have we?"

Caleb Black did not respond. His nostrils flared like those of a wild mustang ready to bolt.

Bridger smiled at Black like an old man smiles at a grandson. Slowly, his face went lax, and the smile disappeared. The impression of age became even more stark.

"It's high time it ended. High time."

McCan said something he had not expected to: "We have him outgunned, Caleb. We can take him alive." But there was no clue from either that he even had been heard.

McCan stepped to the side. Caleb was right; this

was *his* fight. McCan's promise to Maggie couldn't overrule Black's years of obsession. McCan felt peculiarly out of place, like a stranger who has entered a room where lovers embrace. He looked at Black's face: unreadable. He looked at Bridger: what he saw was—surprisingly—relief, and something like satisfaction.

Bridger smiled again, that same, old-man smile.

"Let's do it," he said.

"Let's do it," Black repeated.

Both dropped into a tense stance, legs slightly bent, arms flexed, fingers curved and ready. Bridger's smile vanished and was replaced by a look of determination. McCan heard his own heartbeat, the movement of the horses, the splashing of the creek.

Like blackbirds that move together in answer to a silent signal, both men put their hands to the butts of their pistols.

Black drew and leveled his gun before Bridger cleared the holster. Black clicked back the hammer, his finger tensed on the trigger, and everything stopped, as if in a photograph.

Black aimed his pistol at Bridger's heart, ready to fire, but not firing. Bridger held his own gun pointed to the ground.

"You've done it!" Bridger said. "You outdrew me! *Do it!*"

Black's hand trembled; he bit his lip. He did not fire.

McCan stood to the side, confused.

"*Do it*, damn you!" Bridger shouted. "Isn't this what you've waited for? Think what happened here all those years ago—what I did in this cabin! Think of the mother and the baby I killed! *Why don't you fire?*"

Caleb Black slowly lowered his pistol. "No," he said.

Bridger stood unbelieving. He cursed and raised his pistol.

McCan never remembered drawing and aiming. His shots struck Bridger in the chest, driving him backward through the rotting door, which shattered into splinters as he fell faceup inside the cabin.

McCan went to the outlaw's side. He cradled the old man's head in his hands. Caleb slowly walked up and also knelt beside him.

Bridger was alive, but barely. Weakly, he opened his eyes, locking them on Caleb, then McCan. He smiled, and a thin rivulet of blood escaped the corner of his mouth.

To McCan he said, "You finally learned it. Aim like it's part of your hand. Point like it's your finger."

Then he looked at Black. "It really was high time, Caleb. High time."

Something changed in Evan Bridger's eyes, and he died, his breath a final, slow hiss.

McCan looked at Caleb Black, but Black looked no longer at Bridger. Instead, he gazed at the back wall of the cabin, and McCan followed his stare.

It is a funny thing, McCan later reflected, *what guilt does to a man—how it eats at him even when he denies it, and fills him until he has to let it out however he can.* McCan knew now that Evan Bridger's long-denied guilt at last had found its outlet.

All over the wall hung papers scrawled with pictures, crude as a child's, of women with large eyes and sad faces, and infants clutched in their arms.

Black rose and walked to the horses. He stood there, leaning against the saddle, and McCan thought he saw him cry.

Gently, McCan lowered Bridger's head to the floor and closed the eyes with his fingers. He saw the outlaw's Colt on the floor beside his relaxed hand. He picked it up and checked it. It was empty.

Evan Bridger had engineered his own death as surely as if he had put a bullet into his own brain.

CHAPTER 34

McCan found a board, scratched out the sides of a wash, and buried Evan Bridger as best he could. He pieced together two more boards into a cross, wrote the name of the outlaw on it, and planted it at the head of the grave.

He went to Caleb Black, who still stood at his mount. McCan untethered and slid into the saddle.

"Well?" he said.

"Let's go," Black said.

They left the valley behind and rode into Virginia City. They found a hotel and rented rooms—separate this time, for both men wanted to be alone.

"I'm going to bed early," Black said. "I want an early start back to Jerusha tomorrow."

Inside his room, McCan sat on his bed. It began raining, pelleting the roof and driving in through the open window. McCan did not care.

He lit a lamp and dug from his pocket the little pillbox portrait of Maggie. He looked at it, thinking about the truth he had been able to accept only gradually.

Maggie was not his, and never had been, even in those days when she shared his company. Furthermore, whatever happened to Rodney Upchurch, she never *would* be his. It was Upchurch she loved, live or die. There was just no place for Luke McCan.

He smiled at the irony, then rose and walked to the window. He held the pillbox in his fist, squeezed it, and threw it out into the rain and darkness. Then he found a pad of paper and wrote two notes.

One was to Caleb Black. It said:

Caleb, I cannot stay even the night. I am going back to Timber Creek to report what happened to Evan Bridger and to see if Rodney Upchurch is alive or dead, and then I will be gone. Somewhere else, but I don't know for sure just where. I have my horses, guns, and poker, so I can live. You will see me again, and I wish you well in the marriage you will have.

Luke.

The other was to his sister in Missouri. It said:

Martha—I am somewhat free and have missed you and I think I will see you soon. Just a visit, but one I look forward to. I shall sleep in the barn and be no bother.

Love, Luke.

He folded the letters and put them in envelopes. Then he gathered his hat and saddle bags and walked into the hall. Caleb's note he hung on the latch of Black's room. The other he marked and posted downstairs, and left with the clerk for mailing.

He walked into the downpour to the livery. He saddled his horse and rode away, not looking back, and thus not seeing Caleb Black standing at the window of his room, watching him go.

Black watched until McCan was lost in the rain and darkness. "Good-bye, my old friend," he said. He went to his bed, slid beneath the covers, and in moments was asleep.

LOOK FOR
THE GLORY RIVER—
THE FIRST INSTALLMENT
IN CAMERON JUDD'S
NEW *UNDERHILL*
SERIES!

*Near the Chickasaw Bluffs of the Mississippi River,
just after the turn of the 19th century*

Bush flicked his knife one more time on the piece of
cane, held the cane to his eye, and looked down it.
Good and straight, and cut just below the joint so the
bottom of the cane section was enclosed. Perfect. He
laid the cane section, about a foot in length, aside, and
picked up a straight piece of hardwood already partially whittled into the shape of a pestle, or plunger.

Bush glanced up and around, wondering where Cephas was. He'd been gone too long, already over an
hour beyond their rendezvous time. Bush wondered if
he'd made a mistake and come to the wrong rendezvous point. He thought hard. No. This was the right
place. He and Cephas Frank had rendezvoused at this
same point along the river many a time over the past
six years.

Six years. Hard to believe that much time had gone
by since the dismal, rainy evening they first met at the

burned-out cabin where Bush had dug for the bones of his sister, to no avail. Six years of searching, of question-asking, praying, and hoping, and he was no closer to learning whether Marie Underhill was living or dead.

He whittled on the hardwood plunger a little more, then test-fitted it to the piece of cane. It fit in, sliding all the way to the enclosed bottom, not too loose, not too tight. Perfect so far.

Noise near the river made him look, wondering if Cephas was arriving at last. No, just a possum prowling around lazily. Bush looked around and wondered again what had become of his partner.

Old Cephas. A rather peculiar stranger to him that first day, and now one of the closest friends Bush had ever known, every bit as close as Jim Lusk had been. Bush and Cephas had much in common, despite their different races and backgrounds, and Bush had always thought that was what made them get along with one another so well. Neither fit well into the dominating society around them. Both were far more comfortable in the wilderness than in towns and society, both were capable, natural woodsmen, and both appreciated the privilege of freedom more than most.

And both had lost sisters. That more than anything seemed their strongest common bond. Cephas's sister had died during the raid on the Simpkins cabin and lay buried beneath it. Bush's sister, who could say? Perhaps some of those bones under the cabin had belonged to her. Maybe the raiders who struck the cabin had hauled Marie away. Or perhaps she had already gone from the Simpkins house, on her own or with someone else, before their arrival.

Bush was tired of not knowing, and though he hadn't said anything of it to Cephas, he was beginning to think of giving up. He'd hoped against hope that they'd somehow pick up some bit of Marie's trail, but so far years of effort and countless miles of travel had failed to turn up a thing. And for Bush, hope was beginning to wear thin.

He picked up some hemp fibers he'd gathered and prepared, and began wrapping them tightly around the large end of the plunger he made. What he was up to was something of an experiment, dreamed up years ago by Jean-Yves Freneau, who never had a chance to try it, because his life was cut short by the raid on Coldwater. Bush always wanted to carry out the experiment himself, but only now got around to it.

He looked about for Cephas again. The day was waning. If Cephas didn't come in soon, he probably wouldn't see him this day at all, and Bush would spend the night worrying. They often separated to go on individual hunts and explorations many, but never before had Cephas failed to show up at the designated time and place.

I'm getting to be like an old woman, Bush thought. *Cephas can take care of himself.*

Bush wrapped the pestle until it fit so snugly into the cane section he couldn't muscle it in farther. Good. He popped it out again, then from one of his pouches produced a little wooden container filled with grease. He smeared the grease liberally over the tightly wrapped fibers on the end of the plunger. Then to that end, he attached a little ball of charred tinder. He placed the plunger against the open end of the cane section and pushed it in. Lubricated by the grease, it went in more easily this time, but the fit was airtight.

"Well, let's give your idea a try, Father," Bush said to the spirit of the man who raised him.

He rapidly pushed the plunger into the cane section, giving it a lot of force. Pulling it back up again, but not quite out of the cane section, he rammed it down one more time. Again and again he pushed and withdrew the piston-like plunger, compressing and decompressing the air inside the cane section.

The cane began to grow hot in Bush's hand. It was working!

When his instinct told him to, Bush pulled the piston out of the cane section with a loud popping sound, and to his delight found the tinder glowing and sparking. Jean-Yves Freneau, with that philosophic and scientific mind of his, had been right! Through the compression of air alone, a man could generate enough heat to build a fire.

Bush blew the tinder into a flame and applied it to yet more tinder piled and waiting beside him. As the fire caught, he added kindling sticks, then gradually, larger pieces of wood. The fire burned nicely, a fire created by nothing more than muscle-power and air.

Bush grinned as the flames rose. Jean-Yves Freneau would have been proud to see this.

Above and around, shadows descended. The sun was edging westward over the river. Pleased as Bush was with his successful experiment—and the fact that he now possessed a very practical new fire-making tool—he was still preoccupied with concern for Cephas Frank.

He surely hoped everything was all right.

Three miles downriver, Cephas Frank crouched in the brush on a high bank and looked down on a scene playing out on a roughly made flatboat moored below him. Though this craft, hardly more than a raft with a low-ceilinged, flat-topped shed built in its center, seemed hardly worthy of any kind of name, someone had given it one: *The George Washington* was painted onto the side of the shed.

Three men on the flatboat were talking with a fourth; occasionally some of their conversation would be loud enough for Cephas to hear. What he heard troubled him. As best he could tell, the three men were striking some sort of bargain with the fourth, and the object of the deal was a dark-haired, pretty woman who stood at the door of the shelter. Cephas looked closely at her. Her face was sad. One of the saddest he ever seen.

She turned slightly. Cephas peered more closely at her, and whispered, "Sweet mother of—"

"Well!" a man's voice behind him said. "What've we got here?"

As Cephas began to rise and turn to face two men, who'd come up unheard behind him, the second said, "Looks to me like we got us a nigger poking about where he got no business."

Cephas had laid his rifle on the ground beside him while he watched the flatboat, but picked it up as he rose. He shifted it just a little, ready to bring it up for use if need be.

"Is he right, nigger? You been watching our boat? Or maybe you been eyeing that white woman down there! Ain't right, you know, a darky looking at a white woman. What's your name, darky?"

"I go by Cephas."

"Got you a last name, or are you just one of them one-name slave darkies?"

"He's a runaway. Sure as hell."

"I'm no runaway."

"We supposed to take your word? There might be a reward for you, nigger. You're coming back to the boat with us, and then you can explain why you been up here watching us. And maybe we'll make you pay for staring at our woman. She don't come for free, you know."

Silence. Followed by a sudden charge in the air. One of the intruders cursed and moved at Cephas, who raised his rifle. His position and close quarters in the brush worked against him, though, and he was unable to get the rifle raised before the second man moved in, much faster than the first, and got his hand around the barrel, pushing it away, making it impossible for Cephas to aim.

The first man brought up his arm; there was something in his hand. The arm flashed down, and Cephas felt a jolting, painful thud against the side of his head. He staggered, losing his strength and his grip on the rifle, which was pulled away from him.

He stumbled backward, fighting not to pass out. He saw the glitter of a shiv's blade. His opponents moved toward him.

Cephas put up his arms to fight as the world danced and moved before his unfocused eyes, and a dark numbness began to descend upon him. He went down, and even before he fully passed out, they were upon him, cursing, the shiv rising and then falling, once, twice, three times.

Something's wrong, Bush thought. *Cephas should be here by now. Something's surely wrong.*

He rose and put out the fire he so cleverly built, hefted up his weapons, and set out for Cephas. When they'd split up, Cephas had headed south and he north, so now Bush turned southward.

The farther he traveled the more unsettled he felt. It was just an intuitive feeling, but Bush couldn't shake it off. He searched, called Cephas's name, though not too loudly. Along the river, one never knew who was within earshot, or what kind of response one would receive.

The sun was almost to the horizon. Bush pressed his

search all the harder. Another hour, and he would have to give up and go back to the rendezvous point in hopes that Cephas was merely late.

Ten minutes later, he found the first evidence that something was amiss. A wooden powder horn plug, lying on the ground in a clearing, proof of recent human presence. Bush picked it up and examined it. Cephas's powder horn plug, no question of it. The plug had a distinctive shape and a chip off one side.

Bush examined the clearing and detected that there had been some significant activity here. Branches were bent and broken, grass and young tree sprouts mashed to the ground. A scuffle, maybe.

Soon Bush located evidence that something heavy had been dragged through the brush. There was blood.

Hurrying along in the waning light, following the sign, Bush soon found him. Cephas was on his belly, having dragged himself nearly a quarter of a mile from the clearing where Bush had found the powder horn plug.

"Cephas . . . Lord, Cephas, what's happened to you?"

Bush dropped to his knees beside his partner and carefully rolled him onto his back. The moment he saw Cephas's puffed, bruised face, he knew it was bad. There was blood coming out his nostrils and crusting around his mouth.

"Bush . . . Bush . . . listen to me . . ."

"You shouldn't try to talk, Cephas."

"Listen . . . George   Washington . . . flatboat . . . saw them . . . saw them there, and I saw—" He cut off, blood coming up his throat in a great gush, filling his mouth, choking him.

Bush turned Cephas's head to one side, letting the

blood clear from his throat. "Lie still, Cephas. I got to find us help."

Cephas would not lie still. He pulled his head back to its previous position. "Got to . . . listen . . . brothers . . . it was them . . . saw her, Bush. On the boat . . . George Washington . . . woman . . . saw her . . . the mark . . . I could see it, clear . . . knew she was . . . she had to be . . ."

Cephas was almost unconscious, his words coming harder, making less and less sense. George Washington? What could that mean? Bush was sure his partner was babbling because his mind was failing him as his life drained away.

Bush pulled open Cephas's shirt and winced. Puncture wounds, small and deep, like those a riverman's shiv would inflict. They'd bled much, but were now closed and crusted. Most likely the story was quite different deep inside Cephas, though.

"Cephas, don't die. Don't die." Bush didn't want to weep, but tears came.

"Bush . . . two of them . . . hit me, cut me . . . and they, they . . . she was . . . they was . . ." A new gush of blood came up from inside, cutting his voice off, filling his mouth, spilling over. Cephas's head rolled slowly to the side and his eyes went glassy.

Bush knelt over him and wept like a child. Cephas Frank was dead. Another friend and partner lost, as he had lost Jim Lusk.

Bush buried his partner where he had died, and for all the next day, lingered in the vicinity, numb with grief at the loss of a friend, angry at the world for its unfairness and cruelty, and sorrowful for Cephas Frank himself, his life cut short.

He thought over Cephas's final babblings, trying to

make sense of them. Much of what Cephas had said Bush already forgot—he'd been in such shock at Cephas's condition that most of it had sailed right past him—but some of it, maybe, made sense.

Cephas had probably been trying to tell Bush who hurt him. The "George Washington" reference Bush could make no sense of, but there'd been something about a flatboat, and brothers. "It was them," he'd said. Them. The ones who'd hurt him, he must have meant. Men from a flatboat. A couple of brothers, Cephas's words indicated.

Standing by Cephas's grave, Bush collected his thoughts, then spoke to his departed friend. "I'll not let this pass, Cephas. Somehow I'll find whoever did this to you. I'll see they receive their due punishment, if only from me." Bush's throat grew tighter, emotion filling him. "For three years you and me have roamed, hunting, trapping, fishing, working the river. For three years you've kept my hopes up about Marie when I was ready to give up. You've told me time and again that I should never think her dead until I know she's dead, and that if me and you had switched places, and it was your sister who maybe was still alive out there, somewhere, you'd hunt for her long as you lived." Bush rubbed his eyes. "Well, Cephas, I appreciate all of that, you keeping me going, keeping me thinking that maybe I can find her someday. But three years is a long time, time enough to drain a lot of the hope and spirit out of a man. And now that you're gone, I don't know I've got any spirit left at all, nor any will to keep trying. So I'm going to give up looking for Marie for now. Maybe for good. I'm too weary of it to keep up, and tired of having my hopes rise only to get pulled down again. I'm letting Marie go, Cephas. From now on, the looking I'll do is for the ones who did this to you. And that's one quest I won't fail in. I promise you. I promise."

He took up his rifle and packs, looked for a last time at the grave of another friend and partner, and turned his steps southward.

It was easy now for Bush to understand what had overtaken Jim Lusk in the last days of his life.

Lusk had lost a wife, a greater loss, Bush knew, than that of a friend and partner, but the grief was similar. And with the passing of Cephas went his sole source of encouragement to keep up the seemingly vain search for Marie Underhill, Bush felt a double bereavement.

As he watched himself over passing weeks, he began to wonder if the soul of Jim Lusk had mystically replaced his own.

Bush found he simply wasn't the man he was. He began making mistakes, losing the edge of perfection that always marked his woodcraft. His mind wandered; at times he became lost in areas he'd traveled a score of times with Cephas Frank.

It was just like Lusk had done.

One new thing entered Bush's life that hadn't entered Lusk's in his last days. Bush began to drink, much more than he ever had. He'd never really had much fondness for liquor, drinking it minimally, never getting drunk, and many times taking a simple glass of cold water in honest preference over stronger drinks others clamored for. It was different now. He left the woods behind, began haunting the dives of riverside communities, drinking, brawling, acting and even looking so different from his prior self that he sometimes went initially unrecognized by men he'd met on the river years before.

Bush forgot much of himself as days passed, even stopped thinking about Marie, who'd occupied at least some back corner of his attention almost constantly since that day at Nickajack when he'd pledged to find her, no matter what. But he never forgot what happened to Cephas Frank, and his vow to find and punish his killers.

Bush got it in mind to go to Natchez. There, in the hellholes and dens of infamous Natchez-under-the-hill, he would have a better chance of finding the sort of river trash who would murder a man such as Cephas.

He continued working his way southward, living on what he could kill, and twice, to his astonishment, on what he could steal. These thefts were not large, just a loaf of bread in one case and half a pie in another, but they were atypical of Bushrod Underhill, who'd had honesty drilled into his soul by Jean-Yves Freneau in his earliest days, and reinforced by Jim Lusk and others since.

Bush was half-drunk one late afternoon on a saloon barge that had pulled to shore about halfway between the Chickasaw Bluffs and Natchez, when he found what he was looking for. He'd been seated on a keg at the edge of the barge, looking out across the water and drinking from a dirty pewter cup, when a flatboat came into view up the river. He watched it idly as it drifted along at the speed of the current.

A friendly young boy, son of the owner of the saloon barge, came over to Bush and sat down crosslegged beside him. "Look yonder at them clouds sweeping up," the boy said. "There's going to be a devil of a storm this evening."

"Believe so," Bush said, taking another swallow.

The boy said no more for a while, watching the rising storm, then turning his attention to the same flatboat that Bush had been casually observing.

"George Washington," the boy said.

Bush, frowning, looked down at him. "What'd you say?"

"George Washington. See? It's writ there on the side of that flatboat. I read it off myself." The boy smiled, proud of his literacy in a day when many an older soul than he couldn't read a word.

Bush came to his feet, dropping his cup, staring at the flat-boat. "Lord . . ."

With both heart and mind racing, Bush stared at the flatboat as it neared, wondering if it might swing toward the bank so those aboard it could take advantage of the saloon barge. The boy's father, hoping to stir more business, went to the side of his barge and called across the water, encouraging the flat boatmen to stop in for "fine libation."

A call came back, carrying loud over the water: "Not today, friend! 'Nother time!"

Bush turned to the boy and grabbed his shoulders a little too roughly. The youngster's eyes went wide. "Son, I need a canoe, something I can use to get over to that flatboat."

"Only canoe we got is right yonder, but that belongs to—hey!"

Bush, releasing the boy, had already gone for the

canoe, which sat on one end of the barge, tied upside down. He loosened the ropes and prepared to put it into the water.

The barge owner approached. "You, there! What the deuce are you doing? That's my canoe!"

Bush wheeled, knife in hand, and held it toward the man. "I got to borrow it. I'll bring it back."

"That canoe ain't available for loan."

"Then I'll rent it, damn it! Now you stand aside. Boy, go fetch my rifle and such over yonder. Bring it to me, easy and careful, and don't think of trying any tricks with it."

The boy turned. "Ain't no rifle."

Bush looked. The boy was right—his rifle and packs, left near the place he'd been seated, had disappeared. Some other patron of this floating establishment had made off with them while he was drunkenly unaware.

Taken aback, momentarily unsure of what to do, Bush watched *The George Washington* moving on past in the river. Men stood on the deck. He saw a woman there, too, dimly. One of the men turned to her and pointed at the shelter on the middle of the flatboat. She entered it and Bush saw her no more. One man who had ordered her inside took up a spyglass and looked through it at the people on the shore.

"If my rifle's gone, then it's gone," Bush said. "Mr. Saloon Man, just consider this canoe my compensation for what was stole from me while I was at your fine establishment here." Bush put the canoe into the water and took up the paddle.

A burly fellow with a flintlock pistol beneath his belt came up and said to the barge owner, "You want me to stop him?"

"No," the man said. "This fellow's a madman. Just let him go. Ain't much of a canoe anyway."

Bush pushed away from the barge, turned the canoe in the water, and began paddling toward the flatboat, adding the speed of his own muscle to that of the current, gradually closing in on *The George Washington* as the men on its deck watched him coming.

Bushrod Underhill usually would never have been so reckless as to single-handedly attack a flatboat with no more than a canoe and knife. But it wasn't Bushrod Underhill as he had been. This was Bushrod Underhill transformed and maybe ruined. Bushrod Underhill transformed into something utterly different from the man he'd been before.

The canoe came within talking distance of the flat-boat. A tall man, dark-haired, with a clean-shaven face, called out to him: "Who are you, pilgrim?"

"What? Don't you know me?" he grinned harmlessly, knowing he had to get on the boat, and that it would be almost impossible to do so without permission.

"I can't say I do."

Bush cast his eyes skyward, saying, "It astonishes a man how quick his old friends forget him!"

"We don't know you."

Bush looked heavenward again, the image of an exasperated man, and said, "Surely you recall old Jim!"

Another man, much younger than the prior two, said, "I can't say I do."

Bush shook his head. "Gents, my feelings are nigh to getting hurt. I can't believe you can't remember old Jim Lusk!" He looked back at the nearing storm, clouds whipping in low and close, lightning beginning to flash in the distance. "Can I come aboard?" He glanced left to right, and grinned wickedly. "Got me some money . . . and I hear you got something to sell."

The attitude of the men instantly changed. "Jim!

Now I recall you! Come on up and join us."

Aided by the youngest of the flatboatmen, Bush got the canoe up against the boat and climbed aboard. There were five men aboard besides him, and the unseen woman inside the shelter. All the men appeared to be brothers, their features and coloring quite similar.

It came to Bush's mind that he might not leave this flatboat alive. If he determined that these men, or some of them, had killed Cephas, he intended to do all the damage he could with his knife. He was a good fighter, but five against one was five against one.

A moment of doubt—then he was past it. Tuckaseh had told him once that it's too late to think of dry land once one has already jumped in to swim. And there was some biblical quotation Jean-Yves had been fond of, about not looking back once you've put your hand to the plow.

He grinned and nodded at those around him, trying to look a little drunker than he really was. Best to seem a bit of a buffoon just now, rather than a threat.

"You fellers are all looking healthy."

The one Bush had pegged as the eldest spoke. "Let's end the bilge. We don't know you, though maybe you do know us. We meet a lot of men on this river. We're in business, you see. And if I heard you right, I believe it's business you got in mind?"

Bush stepped back one pace and covertly put his hand on the handle of his knife. "The truth is, I came because I believe I owe a debt to you gentlemen."

"What debt?"

Bush looked from face to face. "The debt I owe at least two of you for killing my partner on back up the river. He was a black man, beat and stabbed to death . . . but before he died, he told me the pair who killed him seemed to be brothers, and he called the name 'George Washington.' "

The older men stared stonily, but the face of the youngest told the story, and a moment later it wouldn't have matter if it hadn't, because he chuckled nervously and said, "That nigger. He's talking about that nigger."

The eldest one swore at the youngest, telling him to keep his mouth shut.

So now it was confirmed. Bush pulled out the knife. "Cephas Frank was my friend and my partner, and I swore above his grave that I'd make the men who killed him pay, no matter what the cost."

The eldest brother produced a pistol and leveled it at Bush. "That cost is going to be quite high for you, sir."

"No," the youngest said, pulling a long knife from beneath his waistcoat. "Don't shoot him. This one's acting like a knife-fighter. Let *me* have him."

The eldest glanced at the others, shrugged, and put away the pistol. "As you please."

With a grin, the young man edged to the low, flat-roofed shelter, which wasn't high enough for anyone above a child's height to stand in. Bush thought of the woman within it. Lying down or sitting, no doubt. Probably watching out a knothole.

If so, she was going to have the privilege of witnessing a death, he thought morbidly. Maybe his own.

"Up on top," the young one said, nodding at the shelter. "Good fighting platform."

"You first."

The challenger put one hand on the shelter top, heaved himself up lithely, and was on the shelter so quickly Bush didn't quite see how he did it. "You next."

Bush, wishing he hadn't drunk so much earlier, gave

it a try, and to his pleasure succeeded. On the shelter, with the storm now almost over them and the river moving faster because of heavy rains that had already fallen to the north, Bush confronted his foe, and readied himself to die.

The young flatboatman made the first lunge. Bush jumped back, then forward, slashing. His blade caught his enemy on the side of the face and laid open a shallow cut.

At first the young man, who obviously considered himself a fine knife fighter, looked shocked. He wiped the blood from his face and backed away. He regained his composure quickly, though, a grin spreading across his face. His teeth were perfect and white, which for some reason made him look all the more dangerous.

He lunged and slashed. Bush dodged back, almost too far, nearly dumping himself over the edge of the flatboat platform to the lower deck. He caught himself just in time. The boatmen whooped and hooted and urged on the knife-flourishing combatants on the platform, which was actually the roof of a shed built in the middle of the big raft-like cargo vessel.

"What's the matter with you, my dear and blooming peavine?" the younger fighter mocked from behind those pearly teeth. "Are you looking for a coward's haven to run to? You'll find naught on this boat! You've bit into the flesh of Beelzebub when you met me! I'm the mud hen of hell's darkest thicket! I'm the very child who put the fork in the serpent's tongue! Waaaauuugh! I'm a screamer! I'm damnation and redemption! I'm brimstone! I'm a gouger! Whoooop! Run from me, coward, while you can!"

"I run from no one," Bush said. "You're nothing but the murderer of a fine man, not fit to boast of anything. As for me, I don't brag. Any boasting to be done my blade does for me."

The pair circled and lunged and feinted and snarled, though neither made contact with the other. Lightning flashed and thunder pealed. On the farthermost shore, trees whipped wildly in the wind and birds cawed and called; dogs barked faintly in the distance. The air was wet and crisp, almost crackling with the energy of the approaching storm. Darkness was falling fast, the river flowing faster.

"I'm seeing some prime dancing, sweethearts, but can you fight?" someone bellowed.

"Cut his gullet!" another yelled. "Show him who's the true Orleans fire-belcher!"

The young man barked like a mastiff and slashed, and Bush danced back suddenly with a red line across his bare chest. The cut was not deep or even painful, but sufficient to make the momentum of the fight shift away from Bush.

For five minutes they danced and dodged and slashed, neither gaining much advantage over the other. If the flatboatman had thought he would have an easy opponent, he learned otherwise. Bush Underhill wasn't easy to kill.

But Bush was worried. Even if he prevailed over this one, there were four others. Short of a miracle, he was a doomed man.

The storm caught up with the flatboat, hard rain gushing down all at once, lightning striking somewhere beyond the far bank. Two more lightning flashes came in fast succession. The first splintered a tree on the closer shore, beside a cabin on the very brink of a badly eroded bank. The second struck farther away, but illuminated a sight that made both combatants break their gaze from one another and look landward: the bank beneath the cabin gave way, sliding with a dull roar into the river, carrying the cabin and dumping it into the water.

Lightning ripped through the sky just as Bush looked back at his opponent. His heart jumped throatward as a monstrous and impossible vision appeared before the flatboat and behind the younger man: a gigantic hand. The great claw reached up from the river, bending down toward the deck and crew, ready to snatch as many men as possible into the river.

The boat jolted hard against something. Timbers moaned and cracked, the boat turned completely about, tilting slightly. The great hand knocked several men to the deck, and suddenly the flatboat tilted the opposite direction.

It wasn't really a hand, Bush realized after the initial shock, but a gigantic tree, broken loose and floating free in the water. It had chanced to reach an unseen sandbar at the same moment as the flatboat. The tree was wedged against the underwater obstruction. Its trunk wrenched in the current so that long branches grappled out across the boat while it slammed hard against the spit of sand.

Bush's opponent unexpectedly screamed. A new flash of lightning revealed to all that the young knife-fighter had just been impaled on a sharp branch of the tree. It poked into his back and out of his belly, crimson and wet, some of his stomach pushed out on its end. The force of the racing flatboat had driven the branch completely through him from behind.

The boat twisted on the sandbar and moved forward again. The knife-fighter's bloody form, lodged on the branch, came at Bush and went past him. Something closed around Bush's middle, picking him up. He yelled and scrambled madly but could find no footing.

The boat moved out from beneath him and the tree

that held him twisted down, turning him sideways and plunging him beneath the dark and cold water.

Bush, caught in the limb of the same tree that had killed his opponent, struggled underwater for a moment, then broke free. He had no idea whether he was upside down or right side up, so he merely flailed and kicked. Moments later, he broke through the surface of the water. He'd somehow washed right over the sandbar and now was free in the river, being pushed helplessly along in the current.

As he turned and twisted, struggling to gain control, he caught intermittent glimpses of the flatboat being wrenched about on the sandbar. Voices cried out frantically; receding, barely-visible figures grappled about on the deck. Then, miraculously, the boat came free of the bar and bumped around it. Twisting back into the main current and down the river, it kept pace with Bush as he washed along—though far off to one side of him—then steadily outpaced him and drifted toward the opposite bank.

The miracle he'd needed had come; he was out of reach of those on the flatboat. But the river was just as likely to kill him.

A branch brushed against him and he grabbed it, but it was far too small to float him. He let it go and swam some more. The flatboat had gone out of sight, though he heard the occasional snatch of a voice carried to him like a wind-borne zephyr.

Bush struggled in the water as his feet and hands went numb and his body began to feel heavy. Muscles cramped all over his body, wracking him with pain.

He knew he was going to die in this river. Dead and gone in his mid-twenties, a life cut short before he even had time to figure out what it was all about.

A log bumped his shoulder and pushed him beneath

the surface. He twisted, kicked, and came up again. The log had already passed by, but, working with the current, he managed to catch up with it and get a hand around a stub where a branch had been. His fingers slipped away and again the log went out of reach, but with another great effort Bush managed to reach it and, this time, hold on.

Pulling himself forward, he hooked his other arm around the log and dragged himself slowly up over it. He relaxed as much as possible, letting the log keep him above water.

Now, he thought, he would just float, loosen his muscles and after a few minutes, see if he could kick to the nearer bank.

The log began to turn beneath him, almost throwing him back into the water. He held on tighter, then looked up just in time to see a big sawyer poking out of the water right at him.

He tried to maneuver the floating log around the sawyer, but he had seen it too late. One log bumped another, and Bush was thrown free, back in the water again.

Despair swept him in. He knew his strength would never last, unless he could reach the bank.

Something made Bush turn his head and look behind him.

Floating at him through the storm was something huge, black, and heavy, rolling like a big wheel in the water, moving too swiftly and taking up far too much river on each side for him to hope to escape it.

He surrendered. No hope now. Whatever this was, it would be on him in a moment, slamming him senseless and pushing him under the water.

He closed his eyes and waited to die.

* * *

Moments later, Bush was thinking: This thing must have a mouth, whatever it is, for I swear I believe it's just swallowed me!

He opened his eyes as his body was thrown up against something rough and hard. He rolled over, splashing into water, then bumped against another hard surface. Debris rushed around him. Then it felt, as sure as the world, as if someone had slapped his face. Not particularly hard, just a flat, wet slap, palm and fingers.

Bush found a handhold and pulled himself farther up onto the hard surface, out of the water. The thing he was in steadied and stopped rolling, floating now at a cock-eyed but steady angle. Looking around in nearly pitch blackness, broken sporadically by lightning flashes, Bush suddenly made sense of it all.

He was inside that cabin he'd seen fall off the bluff. The deuced thing had floated down the river, and somehow he'd gotten inside of it!

As best he could guess, the cabin must have rolled over him in just the right way to draw him in through a door or window. He laughed at the absurd luck of it—moments from death, and he was rescued by a floating cabin!

The cabin twisted sideways and something hit him hard on the side of the head. He caught it—a three-legged stool. He saw it drop, in the brief white moment of a lightning flash, into the water below him, and float about, trapped like Bush himself inside the cabin walls. A stout cabin, this one. Obviously spiked together instead of merely notched.

Bush scooted up farther; he was somewhere at the top of an inside wall, just under the edge of the roof. He bettered his handhold, tried to wedge himself as securely as he could, and hoped the house wouldn't roll over again.

It did. The wall to which he clung suddenly pitched downward, dipping into the water and pulling him with it. Then he was out, looking down at the water again, losing his handhold, and falling into the murky wet.

Something fleshy and soft was next to him. He pushed the thing away as the cabin rolled over yet again, then resettled.

Bush was half in, half out of the water. Lightning flared, and he found himself looking into the face of a man who stared back at him but did not see him, for he was dead, the back of his head crushed like a dropped egg. For a moment Bush thought maybe this was the knife-fighter, washed free of the stabbing branch, but it wasn't. The face was different.

Bush pushed the corpse away, disgusted, and scrambled back up the wall again.

The house moved along, rolling no more, though it did twist continually. Bush kept an eye out for the corpse, as if by its own power it could climb up the wall and slap him again like before.

The cabin leveled somewhat as it moved down the river and Bush was able to position himself more steadily. He noticed, however, that the cabin was also riding lower in the water. Before long it would sink, and take him down with it.

At length the cabin angled up enough to bring its puncheon floor, which was spiked to the base logs of the wall, mostly out of the water. Several puncheons were missing; through the gaps he saw the sky go white with each lightning flash. He would work his way out through that opening, climb atop the cabin, and keep his eye open for some alternative support, before the cabin went fully under.

Bush began to climb. He made slow but steady progress, then slipped on the wet wall logs and slid into the water again.

Solidity gave way beneath him and he went down, falling out a submerged window into the cold river below. For a few moments he was wedged in the window, competing for space with something else—the corpse! Then he was through, but found himself under the cabin, and stuck.

He struggled to find a way out from under, but part of his clothing was stuck on some protrusion from the cabin, keeping him below water level. He ached for air, struggled for freedom, and at the last possible moment before the surrounding blackness became unending, the cabin rolled again, pulling him up and out of the water and freeing him from whatever had trapped him.

He gasped, and sucked in huge, welcome breaths. Suddenly, he was tossed into the water again. But as he fell it seemed to him that the eastern bank was not nearly as far away as before. Blindly, he began to swim, realized he was going the wrong way, then turned in the current and pulled himself in the other direction. He swept downriver much more swiftly than he managed to move across it.

Farther ahead in the river, the cabin gave one more roll, wrenched into pieces at last, and vanished. He kept swimming. The bank seemed no closer. He was growing very, very tired.

Bush walked in darkness through a light rain that had begun in the wake of the storm, with no clear memory of having made it to the bank. He was weak, sore, lost, and very disoriented.

He was also weaponless and shoeless; his footwear had come off sometime during his river ordeal. Staring across the river, he looked for the flatboat he had fallen from, but saw nothing. Too dark. Eventually, the rain stopped, the clouds opened to let through the moon, and the broad river shimmered with reflected light. Still no flatboat visible, just assorted floating trash and refuse discarded by the storm.

As bad luck would have it, Bush had washed onto an unpopulated area. Not a cabin was in sight, not a distant glimmer of a settlement or camp—nothing but black Mississippi forest.

Finally Bush quit walking, realizing he'd best wait until daylight and hope for aid from some passing boat. He'd build a fire on the shore, see if he could snare a fish or roust up some other game come morning, and make his way downriver however he could. He'd not gone more than twenty feet when he caught a glimmer of light coming from deeper in the woods. He peered closely. A campfire? It appeared so.

Stepping gingerly because he was barefooted, Bush began moving toward the light, pushing aside branches and brambles, wincing when his foot trod on a stone or burr. The light grew brighter and bigger and soon he began to smell the delicious scent of cooking meat. He listened for voices but heard none. Either the campers were not talking, or there was only one.

Bush stopped, panting. His strength was nearly gone. Whoever started the fire, he hoped they were friendly, and wouldn't be overly startled to see a battered, half-clothed figure such as himself appear.

When the campfire was close enough that its smoke stung his eyes and the smell of the cooking meat made his stomach rumble, Bush cleared his throat and called, "Hello, the camp! Hello! I want to come in, if I may."

No reply came. Bush cleared his throat again and repeated himself, only louder.

Still nothing. Could the fire have been started by lightning, with no one about at all? It didn't seem likely. Not a confined, controlled blaze like that one. Then he sniffed the cooking meat again and knew that the fire had to be man-made. Lightning didn't spit-cook squirrels.

A burst of light-headedness caused Bush to stagger. He leaned against a tree and decided he would have to take his chances and go on in even without permission.

"I'm coming in . . ." His voice was weaker. "I'm a friend . . . I'm coming in."

He advanced, reaching the edge of the woods and

the small clearing where the fire burned. Pausing, he looked about for whoever was camped here, and saw no one.

A mystery indeed, but Bush wouldn't try to solve it. Feeling he might pass out at any time, he walked into the clearing and slumped down near the fire. He was intensely weary, almost too tired even to eat. The scent of the meat was too rich to be ignored, however, and he took the squirrels from the fire, waited until the meat was cool enough to eat, and took a bite.

When he was sated, he tossed the remnants aside and lay out flat on the ground, drifting quickly into a deep slumber.

What awoke him he could not say. His eyes opened; he was facing the fire, but it had mostly burned down. Red embers, spewing smoke and sparks.

Bush was not alone. He felt it.

Sitting up, he sucked in his breath, a reaction to an army of pains that marched up and down his battered body in a short span. Slowly he twisted his head and looked into the darkness just outside the glow of the fire.

Somebody out there. Watching.

Bush rolled over slowly and sat straight up, then came to his feet unsteadily.

"Your camp, I reckon," he said into the darkness.

No response.

"I ate the meat you'd roasted. I'm sorry."

Still nothing.

"I'm hurt . . . got knocked off a flatboat in the storm, and nearly drowned."

Nothing. Silence.

"Is there anybody there?"

The darkness itself seemed alive and ominous.

"If there's somebody there, I'd sure be obliged if

you'd show yourself. I'm unarmed. I'm no threat."

The darkness moved; a piece of it advanced. Not quite fully into the light, but just into the fringes of it. A ghostly, black figure, hard to discern.

"Howdy," Bush said, honestly wondering if it was, in fact, a ghost he was seeing.

The figure held its silence. Bush squinted and tried to see him better. Or was it a man at all? So vague was the image that Bush could not even discern the sex.

"My name's Underhill," Bush said. "Bushrod Underhill. Most just call me Bush for short."

No answer.

"Please, friend, I'd like to ask you to come more into the light if you would. I can't see you well enough to tell a thing about you."

The figure did not move for a moment, but then stepped forward.

Bush stared at the strangest human being he'd seen, either in the world of white men or red. Tall, gaunt, the man had black hair that hung thickly around his narrow face and past his shoulders, as unkempt and uncut as Samson's. The beard was just as long, reaching to the middle of his chest, and black as the river depths by night.

His nose was narrow and protruding, his eyes intensely dark and indefinably strange. Almost unblinking—yes, that was the strangeness of them. They hardly blinked, just gazed ceaselessly.

The clothing was as black as the hair and beard. Loose, dirty trousers, a bulky black coat over an equally colorless waistcoat, and if the shirt had ever been white, it was now dirtied to an indistinct buff.

"Sir, I tell you again that I'm sorry I ate your meat."

The man did not speak.

"I'll be glad to pay you for it, sir, as soon as I can

get my hands on money. I've lost all my possessions, you see. They're still on the flatboat I had the misfortune to be knocked off of, and the boat is no doubt long down the river by now."

The figure moved to one side and slowly bent over until he was seated on his haunches. An uncomfortable looking position, but it didn't seem to bother the stranger.

"Sir, do you speak English?"

The man, who, with his long coat draping past his knees, seemed to be floating on air, still said nothing.

Bush asked him his name in French, to no avail, then dug fragmented German out of the dustiest memories of his days with Jean-Yves Freneau, and repeated his question. Bush even asked in Cherokee. Still no reply.

Bush sat down again, watching the man mistrustfully, thinking him surely the oddest living being on the river. Why did he not answer? Was he deaf?

Bush shifted his position so that he could keep the man in the corner of his eye without staring openly at him, but within minutes the man rose and moved around to face Bush again, with no look of apology about doing so. Bush grinned at him, hoping to earn one in return. He didn't.

The remainder of the night seemed longer than two. Bush didn't dare sleep with this stranger watching him endlessly, saying nothing, looking malevolent with those dark and probing eyes. The pair of them remained as they were, each watching the other in silence. Bush, thinking he must have roused up a forest demon of some sort, scanned through all the Cherokee legends he could recall to see if he could find a match. Nothing quite did. He maintained the fire and made sure he always kept the stranger in sight.

By the pitch-black minutes of pre-dawn, Bush was

mentally exhausted by the extended staring game, and thought it might be better if he abandoned the safety of firelight and heat to take his chances in the forest alone. But with daylight so close, he had developed a superstitious curiosity about what would happen to this vampirish creature come sunrise. Would he vanish like smoke? Retreat into some cavern or hollow tree?

Bush had actually dozed off when the first rays of morning came streaming over the horizon. The stranger, who had been seated on the ground on the opposite side of the fire, suddenly came to his feet, walked to the edge of the clearing, and faced the rising sun. Bush, startled awake, watched him closely.

The man raised his hand skyward, lifted his face toward the clouds, and bellowed, "I thank you, oh Father, for the morning, and I thank you, oh Father, for life and sun and survival through the night. And I thank you, oh Father, for my new companion Mr. Underhill, who you have sent to me for his good and mine. All praise to Father, Son, and Holy Ghost. Amen."

The man turned so quickly that Bush jumped to his feet, expecting to see a pistol come out from under his coat. But the man was empty-handed, and extended those empty hands his way. "Mr. Underhill, I welcome you to my camp. And there is no need to apologize for having eaten my meat. What I have is given me not to hoard but to share. And I'm very sorry about my rude silence. I'd vowed to the Lord that I'd be silent until day, you see, and was simply fulfilling what I'd promised."

Bush was so taken aback to hear a voice coming out of the raven-like man that he hardly knew how to reply. "Sir, who are you?"

"My name is Moses Zane."

"Zane . . . I've heard that name before, sir. You're

a preacher, I think, one my late partner, a free black man name of Cephas Frank, told me of. You're the man folks say can—"

"Can summon up the devil himself and by the power of God make him dance at my command? Or so people say. Yes, I'm that same Moses Zane." He smiled, and seemed a little less odd for it. "And now, Mr. Underhill, how about you and I enjoy a bit of breakfast?"

From behind a tree Zane produced a large leather pouch, and from it pulled half a loaf of hardened but unmolded bread, a hunk of cheese, some nuts, jerked beef, and even a small jug of cider. To Bush it looked like a king's feast.

Zane fished out two crockery cups, scratched and lacking handles. He uncorked the cider and poured some into each cup.

"You do enjoy cider, Mr. Underhill?"

"Yes sir."

"Good, for I have no other beverage to offer you, unless you want to try to find some pure water after such a terrible storm as the mighty Lord sent us last night. I don't think you'll have much success if you do, as much mud as was stirred up." He took a small sip of his own cider while handing Bush the other cup.

"What kind of preacher are you, Mr. Zane?"

"My confession, do you mean? I'm Methodist by doctrine, though at the moment I'm not a part of any official circuit or under the authority of any church structure other than the one true and universal church of Almighty God." He sipped his cider again. "In short, Mr. Underhill, I've been put out of the ministerial fold and must make my way as an independent. Are you hungry, Mr. Underhill?"

"I could eat the very grease off a wagon axle."

"Well, I hope you'll find my fare, such as it is, better than that." Zane distributed the food. A very different man he seemed now from the silent, looming vampire he had been in the darkness. "I normally eat rabbits and squirrels and other small game, saving this food for those times I enjoy the pleasure of human companionship."

"You're alone a lot?"

"Never. My God is always with me. But in the sense in which you meant the question, yes. I'm alone quite often."

"May I ask why you'd told the Lord you would hold silent until morning?"

"Certainly. In my prayers yesterday, I implored the Lord to see to my aid in my time of distress and give me guidance. There came to me at sundown the strongest impression that I should remain silent until sunrise, and during that silence I would find the help I needed. So I made my promise to my Father, and was bound to keep it until the sun came up." Zane ate a handful of nuts.

"What 'time of distress' are you talking about?"

"I was put off here, Mr. Underhill. A crew of keelboatmen found my company to be intolerable. They were not agreeable to hearing the truth that changes souls."

"So you prayed for help. No offense, preacher, but I don't see the Lord has answered your prayer."

"Of course He has! You've come."

"I just fell off a flatboat, sir." Zane needed to know no more than that. "I rode some distance down the water in a cabin that'd come off the bank and was floating down the river with a corpse in it. That cabin rolled right over me in the water and swallowed me like that Jonah fellow with his big fish. I don't know quite how I got out without drowning."

"You were protected in order to be sent to me. And now we must decide what to do now that you've come."

"I know what I have to do," Bush said. "I have to move down the river and look for somebody." He didn't intend for the men who'd killed Cephas Frank to escape him.

"And so we can see providence at work! It happens I need to head downriver myself."

"You may not have noticed, Reverend, but I got no boat. I'm afoot just like you. I ain't even got shoes! I lost my boots in the river."

"I have an extra pair of boots in my pouch. They pinch my feet, but may do better for you."

Indeed they did. Moments later Bush was admiring a pair of boots finer than those he had lost, fitted nicely over his feet. If Zane was peculiar, he was also generous.

Zane said, "I have a proposition for you, Mr. Underhill. You and I will remain together for now and see if we can't find some good passage down the river. Your company and protection will be welcome to me."

It was absurd. Bush couldn't be hampered by company as he tried to track down Cephas's killers, but the preacher had him hooked as a partner for now simply because Bush felt indebted to him for the boots, and he certainly had no money to pay for them. So he heard himself saying, "Well, I reckon we can travel together—for a time."

"Good! Then let's be off, shall we?"

"Where to?"

"Down to the river. Providence has already sent you to me by way of the river. Let's see what else might come floating along."

*   *   *

As they broke camp, Bush made the pleasing discovery that Moses Zane owned a good flintlock rifle, an almost equally good pistol, two fine knives, and a hatchet. They had been out of sight before, tucked away behind the same tree that had concealed the leather supply bag.

"Please, take the weapons with my blessing," Zane told him. "I make them a gift to you. I hate the cursed things. I rarely use them except to occasionally kill small game, such as those squirrels you found on my fire. Most of what I eat is either fish I catch, food good people along the way give me, or rabbits and such I snare."

Bush was astonished that a man would give away such fine weaponry to a near stranger. "Sir, I don't think I can take such a gift as this."

"Nonsense! It's my pleasure to give you the guns, and it should be yours to take them. You lost what you had in the river, I'd be willing to wager—though don't take that literally. I don't favor wagering."

After they had hiked about two miles, the preacher pointed to something Bush had just spotted himself—something caught in tangled brush on the bank. Bush trotted over and found a dugout canoe trapped there. Just the right size for two men.

"God provides!" Zane declared.

Bush reached into the canoe and pulled out an odd item: a dented old hunting horn. Putting it to his lips, he tested it, sending a piercing blast across the water. "Has an unusual sound to it. Clearer and louder than most. Wonder how it came to be in there?" he mused aloud, examining the instrument.

"For a reason, I'm sure. Maybe it will prove to be something I can make use of in some way." Zane looked at the horn and rubbed his chin. "You know,

I think perhaps there is a good use for this instrument. I can use it to sound the call for my meetings. Here, let me try a blow on that."

Bush handed the horn to Zane, who drew in his breath and blew, with pathetic results. With greater effort, he tried again, doing a little better this time.

Suddenly Zane changed. His eyes bulged, his face reddened, and his mouth fell open. The horn dropped from his fingers. Bush went to Zane's side as the man began to collapse slowly to the ground, hand on his chest as he gasped for air.

"Preacher, what's wrong with you?"

"Back . . . away from . . . the river . . ." He collapsed.

Bush swept the man up in his arms and ran.

Zane sat slumped on a rock beneath a spreading, moss-draped tree, looking at the ground and breathing deeply. "Thank God," he whispered. "That time I didn't know if I would make it through."

"What happened?" Bush asked.

"My lungs," Zane replied softly. "Since my boyhood I've struggled with it. My wind sometimes is cut off, my lungs seem to close, and I struggle to draw my breath. An attack of Satan, who always tries to silence me."

Bush looked up and down the preacher's gaunt frame, studying the sallow, narrow face. He looked like someone who had known weakness and sickness all his life. It was no surprise that he was asthmatic.

Zane lifted his gaze and looked gratefully at Bushrod. "Had you not been there, my friend, I might have never breathed again."

"I didn't do a thing," Bush said. "You commenced breathing again on your own."

"Because you carried me away from the river,"

Zane said. "There seem to be times and places that cause it to happen. Excitement, sorrow, fear can all bring it on. And being near rivers can do it as well, though not all the time. Generally, I'm quite able to function normally, or at the very least to have only minor difficulties. This one was . . . different." He shuddered and looked down again. Despite the preacher's apparent tendency toward religious bravado, it was evident to Bush that this man was thoroughly shaken by what happened.

"Reverend, has it crossed your mind that maybe you ought to find some place other than the river country to do your preaching? There's some folks who can't do well for their health in certain places, certain kinds of air. I knew a man once who'd break out in red patches every time he'd walk through a copse of maples, and get wheezy in the chest if ever he breathed air from a cave."

"It's here I belong, Mr. Underhill. Nowhere else. And I've never suffered such an attack while preaching. I believe I'm protected then."

"I wish you'd call me Bushrod instead of 'Mr. Underhill.' "

"Very well, Bushrod. And you may call me Moses." And he went straight into another asthmatic attack. Bush hustled him farther away from the river until his breathing again settled.

Bush grinned at the preacher when he was well again, but he wasn't happy at the moment. He ached to continue his pursuit of *The George Washington* and its murderous crew, but suddenly this puny preacher was, as it were, tossed into his lap, giving gifts and making Bush feel obliged to him. He had no impression that Zane was trying to manipulate him—but he'd hooked him all the same. He couldn't abandon a man who might smother to death at any given moment.

It appeared that, for the short term, he had himself a traveling companion.

The fire was strong, and in its warm glow Zane didn't look nearly as weak and pale as he had in the white, color-stealing light of morning.

"So, Bushrod, where are you from?"

Bush didn't really want to enter that rather complicated history. "A lot of places. I was born near what's now Nashville, in Tennessee."

"I see. I've never been there. What profession do you follow?"

"I've been a lot of things. Mostly now I hunt, work the river some, flatboating and all. And live off the land."

"I see. Sounds, in some ways, like my life. Much wandering."

"Yes, there's that."

"Do you have family?"

"No wife. My parents are dead. I have a sister— had a sister."

"She's dead?"

Bush paused, looked down. "Yes."

"I'm sorry. Was she a Christian?"

"I never had the chance to know her much, preacher. We were separated early on in life."

"You've had some sorrows, my friend."

"I have."

"How did you become separated?"

Bush was just opening his mouth to respond when the brush on the far side of the camp clearing opened, and a man stepped out of the woods with a rifle raised, aiming it squarely at Moses Zane's head.

CAMERON JUDD
THE NEW VOICE OF THE OLD WEST

*"Judd is a keen observer of the human heart
as well as a fine action writer."*
— *Publishers Weekly*

THE GLORY RIVER
Raised by a French-born Indian trader among the
Cherokees and Creeks, Bushrod Underhill left the dark
mountains of the American Southeast for the promise of
the open frontier. But across the mighty Mississippi, a
storm of violence awaited young Bushrod—and it would
put his survival skills to the ultimate test...
0-312-96499-4___$5.99 U.S.___$7.99 Can.

SNOW SKY
Tudor Cochran has come to Snow Sky to find some
answers about the suspicious young mining town. And
what he finds is a gathering of enemies, strangers and
conspirators who have all come together around one
man's violent past—and deadly future.
0-312-96647-4___$5.99 U.S.___$7.99 Can.

CORRIGAN
He was young and green when he rode out from his family's Wyoming ranch, a boy sent to bring his wayward
brother home to a dying father. Now, Tucker Corrigan was
entering a range war. A beleaguered family, a powerful
landowner, and Tucker's brother, Jack—a man seven years
on the run—were all at the center of a deadly storm.
0-312-96615-6___$4.99 U.S.___$6.50 Can.

TERRY C. JOHNSTON

THE PLAINSMEN

THE BOLD WESTERN SERIES FROM
ST. MARTIN'S PAPERBACKS

COLLECT THE ENTIRE SERIES!

SIOUX DAWN
92732-0 _____ $5.99 U.S. _____ $7.99 CAN.

RED CLOUD'S REVENGE
92733-9 _____ $5.99 U.S. _____ $6.99 CAN.

THE STALKERS
92963-3 _____ $5.99 U.S. _____ $7.99 CAN.

BLACK SUN
92465-8 _____ $5.99 U.S. _____ $6.99 CAN.

DEVIL'S BACKBONE
92574-3 _____ $5.99 U.S. _____ $6.99 CAN.

SHADOW RIDERS
92597-2 _____ $5.99 U.S. _____ $6.99 CAN.

DYING THUNDER
92834-3 _____ $5.99 U.S. _____ $6.99 CAN.

BLOOD SONG
92921-8 _____ $5.99 U.S. _____ $7.99 CAN.

ASHES OF HEAVEN
96511-7 _____ $6.50 U.S. _____ $8.50 CAN.